I'll Fly Away

Maya Winston

Published by Trellis Publishing, 2021.

I'LL FLY AWAY

MAYA WINSTON

Ruby had always been a curious child. She often peeked at the English from beneath her lashes when they would pass by her buggy in their cars, talking on their cell phones. She wondered what it would be like to be free like those girls were. She knew the feeling of the sun on her face and arms, but what would it feel like on her legs? What would it be like to wear a shirt that even showed her stomach, as she had seen some of the girls from outside her community did during the summer? Or even more daringly, what about a bikini at the water's edge? What if she could choose her own way in the world, without being limited by her community? It had always seemed so unfair that she would be so stifled in her pursuits and those English girls didn't even seem to appreciate what they had in their freedom. They took it for granted, of that much she was sure.

The idea of *Rumspringa* had always been one that fascinated her. Older children of the community were given time, sometimes years to explore a life outside of her Amish faith and community. They were allowed the freedom that she had always craved. And then, to her utter shock, most of them made the choice to come back! She would always shake her head at these baptisms. She couldn't understand why someone would choose a life of limitations and strict rules, when they were given the option to leave it all behind.

It was true that in leaving the community, a person would be leaving their family and friends and choosing an unfamiliar life, but that was the adventure she craved. Missing her parents wouldn't be worth staying under the thumb of her community. She believed in God, of course, and she was as faithful as she was expected to be in her activities, but there was something always screaming in the back of her head that she wanted to experience more.

"Ruby, where are you, child?" Her father's voice pulled her from her thoughts. She didn't answer immediately, wanting just another moment of peace with her own thoughts. "Ruby?"

"Out here, Father," she finally answered reluctantly. "I'm back with the babies."

Ruby loved spending time with the calves after all of the milking was done. She found their innocence sweet and their affection refreshing. Her family members loved each other, but weres not physically affectionate. She craved that contact, even if she had to get it from the calves and horses that lived on their farm. It made her unusual to love the animals so much, rather than treating them as strictly instruments and tools, but she was used to the way that she was different and didn't think that she could function any other way.

Her father rounded the corner with a stern look on his face. "They are calves, Ruby, not babies." Her father couldn't understand the way that she doted after what he saw as nothing more than working parts of the farm. "Why are you hiding back here when there is work to be done?"

"I wasn't hiding, Father. I was doing the milking and then feeding the babies."

"You aren't arguing with me, are you, young lady?"

"No sir." Ruby hung her head as she was scolded. She was beyond frustrated with the way she was always expected to behave according to her parents' rules.

"Go on in and help your mother with the chores. She has been waiting for you for nearly an hour. It doesn't take an hour to feed the calves."

Ruby wanted to argue and rage, but she simply nodded and walked past her father toward the house. She saw him shake his head out of the corner of her eye, but only looked straight ahead to avoid his judgmental gaze. She told herself that she only needed to hold on for a couple more days until *Rumspringa* and then she would be free to experience life in her own way. After all, she was practically an adult now. A seventeen year old woman should not have to hang her head like a child simply because her father scolded her. She knew that not all of the families in her community were as strict as hers, but she had been dealt a certain hand, and she was ready to move on to a new game.

She lived in one of the few Amish communities in the area where the children were allowed to completely leave the community if they chose to. Many of her fellows stayed at home and simply lived with fewer rules, but there was always a handful that would choose to go outside, find a place to live and experience life as the English did. Ruby's parents refused to allow her to completely leave their home, but they had no choice about allowing her to live without restrictions. It was the way that it had always been and it would be for her. She knew that many of the older generation, including her father, saw *Rumspringa* as a chance for young women like her to find a husband for when they chose to be baptized and remain with the Amish community, however, she wasn't going to treat it that way. She played her part well and he didn't know, but the second that she could, she was going to leave to stay with friends if she could, and she would not be returning, no matter how much her parents would insist. She smiled to herself as she walked toward the house. It was almost time for her to begin living her life the way she had wanted to since she was old enough to know the difference.

* * *

One of the expectations that her father had of Ruby was for her to be an active participant in the community. This meant that since she was old enough to do so, she had not only helped out with caring for her neighbors, but she also volunteered to be on committees and help with large-scale social events that were to be put on for the community by the community members. Currently she was a member of the committee that was organizing community-wide meals and social gatherings. She actually loved her role there, because she was able to share her ideas without fear of being reprimanded for doing so. Not all of her ideas were adopted, but at least she was able to use her voice.

The events often fell on holidays or coincided with different harvests, so there was usually an event to plan at every biweekly meeting.

The current event that they had been working on was happening that very evening, so Ruby was expected to spend the entirety of the day in town setting up, helping with last minute details, and making sure that all was to going to run smoothly. It was such an exciting time for her that she found her mind wandering to wanting to do something like this when she finally joined the English community. "Party planning" is what she believed they called it. She was good at planning and it made her smile, which not a lot of things did these days.

This particular committee was actually rather large. There were several children just a couple of years younger than her that were willing to do just about anything that was asked of them. There were also four young adults, including Ruby, that were on the eve of embarking upon the *Rumspringa* phase of their lives. They had all been best friends since early childhood. And finally there were a handful of adults that participated. Ruby could never keep track of how many because they came and went with each meeting. She was never sure who would be at each meeting. It was a traditional set-up, as the adults mentored the young adults and the young adults mentored the children. It was the way of their community that the young learned from their elders, and it was no different in the case of the committees on which Ruby served.

This had been her favorite event to plan in a long time, because it was a combination of a celebration of an elder's birthday and the marking of the harvest. Big parties like that always took a great deal of work, but they kept her busy and were always a fun time during the event itself. It was also significant because it was the last event that she would be planning before she started her journey away from the community. So even though no one else around her knew it, she was treating the dinner ad celebration as her farewell to the constraints of her Amish life.

She arrived at the community hall late morning and started right in on the work that needed to be done. Decorations were often overlooked as being important, but she very much wanted to dress up the hall, so she had taken it upon herself to be in charge of the decorations. She recruited the other participants of her age and they spent weeks gathering all that they would need. Now that the event was that evening, they were working hard executing the plans that they had come up with during the planning phase. The plan was to work through the lunch hour to make sure that the hall would be ready for that evening.

As the clock struck twelve o'clock, Ruby was making her way down to where her three best friends, Annabelle, Phillip and Donna, were stringing up the lanterns that they would be using to light up the dinner in the hall basement in just a couple of hours. The rest of the tasks were complete, and she breathed out a sigh, knowing that all they had left to do was to finish the hall decorations. That would only take another hour or so, and they would be ready well ahead of when the older folks would arrive to begin the cooking of the food that they would all have for dinner that evening.

As she came near to rounding the corner into the hall, she heard excited voices.

"Annabelle, don't be nervous, it is going to be so much fun!" Phillip said with a chuckle.

"But it's going to be so different," Annabelle answered quietly.

"That's the point, Annie," Donna answered. "Think about it. Living amongst the English is going to give us a chance to live another life before we decide if we're going to settle down here."

Ruby froze before entering the hall. They were speaking of *Rumspringa*. She listened intently as the conversation continued.

"I know, but I'm just thinking that maybe I should stay here and visit you." Annabelle's voice was tentative. Their friend Donna was a force of nature, and Annabelle trying to pull out of any plan would not be met by her happily.

"Listen, the fact that our parents have agreed to allow us to live outside the community at all is a miracle, especially considering mine think that *Rumspringa* should be all about finding the man that I am planning to marry. We aren't going to be far from the community, and you know that Phillip's cousin will have a car for us to drive."

"Oh my," Annabelle groaned, "I forgot about the car." This was met by a hearty laugh by both Phillip and Donna. They all knew that Annabelle was the worrier of the group and sometimes her reactions were met with frustration, but more often than not, they were a source of amusement.

"Listen," Phillip said calmly, "why don't you come with us and try it. If you don't like it you can come back. You at least have to try staying at the apartment for a few weeks before you decide."

Ruby couldn't believe her ears. Her friends were all going to be leaving the community and living together in an apartment. It was astounding. Why didn't she know anything about this? She felt a surge of envy, followed by anger. Why hadn't they included her in their plans? With her face burning, she rounded the corner and stalked toward her friends.

"Hey Ruby," Phillip said cautiously, "something wrong with the lanterns?"

She looked up and around her for the first time since entering the room, and her anger faded just a little. "No. Actually they look amazing," she said. "I'm just wondering why you guys never told me about your plans to leave me here all alone, while you're off living in some English apartment."

The three exchanged glances. Obviously they knew that this would be her reaction. The four of them had been best friends since they were barely walking.

"We would have mentioned it sooner, Ruby, but we knew how your parents feel about it." Phillip was obviously pained. "If it were up to me you would come along, but of course it isn't. Some of the elders were speaking with all of our parents, and yours were the only ones that stated there would be no chance that they would allow you to choose to leave the community. All the rest said that they would leave it up to us, but yours said that they knew what was best for you, and that they would be making the decision. They said that they couldn't stop you from living outside of Amish rules, but that they could at least shelter you from what you would find living outside of the community."

"It's sort of sweet in a twisted, controlling way," Donna added.

"Donna, that is not helping," Annabelle said gently.

Suddenly the anger left her like air from a balloon. She let out a huff and slumped into a nearby chair. "I can absolutely believe that they said all that. This is terrible. All I've wanted forever is to get out of here, but at least I have always had you guys. Now not only am I going to be stuck here, but you guys are going to be leaving me too." She felt her eyes burning with tears of frustration.

"Look," Phillip said, grabbing her hands and pulling her to her feet, "we will be at my cousin's place. He says there is plenty of room. You have to come and stay with us whenever you can get away. I know for a fact that your parents agreed with letting you visit us over certain weeks and weekends." He smiled and squeezed her hands again. Their eyes held for a moment and she felt her insides melt a bit at the intensity of his gaze. "Come on Ruby, smile for us. Look at what an outstanding job I did on these lanterns, all by myself."

"Umm, hardly by yourself, Phillip," Donna answered forcefully.

Ruby couldn't help but laugh at the incredulity on Donna's face. For years Phillip had always known how to get a rise out of his three best friends, and he often did so to cheer up another that might have been having a tough time. It worked every single time for Ruby. She couldn't deny that having her friends' support was a huge part of what made her life in the community at least bearable, if not enjoyable.

"It isn't ideal, Ruby, but it's better than nothing," Annabelle said once Ruby's laughter had died down. "You might even be happier," she added.

"No, you would be happier. I heard the conversation you were having before I came in. You don't even want to go." She couldn't keep the bitterness out of her tone. "How ironic is it then that I want to go and can't, when you can go but won't?"

"I know, Ruby, I'm sorry." Annabelle did sound genuinely upset by Ruby's words.

"It's not your fault, Annie," Ruby said on a sigh. "I shouldn't blame you. I'm just so restless here."

"Well," Phillips said grandly, "then let's enjoy tonight's party and get prepared, because tomorrow everything changes for us, no matter where we lay our heads to sleep!"

* * *

Phillip's words on that last night before their *Rumspringa* turned out to be quite prophetic. When Donna, Phillip and Annabelle left to claim their spots in Phillip's cousin's apartment, Ruby was left behind living much the same way that she had been living up until that time. There were some subtle differences where she was not held to the same rigorous expectations as before, but the scenery had remained very much the same. The breathing room that she had gained had not yet given her what she wanted, a chance to escape her confines. That was going to be coming today. She was packing her bags to head into the English world to spend a whole week with her friends. No rules, no expectations, no one looking over her shoulder and judge her motives for every move that she made.

Ruby felt practically giddy as she finished packing her items. She was going to be meeting her friends on the edge of town and riding in a car. A car, of all things! This would be a weekend of firsts; she knew that to be true. She wanted to catch up with her friends and find out how life had been treating them over the past two months. And she wanted to finally find that freedom that she was so craving. She wanted to not just breathe, but gulp free air.

Her parents had said good-bye to her earlier that day, which made the task of preparing to go that much simpler. She had listened that morning, for longer than she cared remember, to both of them giving her warnings about the dangers and sins out in the English world. She had heard all about how her friends could possibly now be tainted and how she must not trust anyone outside of the community. On and on it had gone. When they finally left for the day, she had rushed in and started packing right away. She didn't want to take the chance that they would come back and start it again.

She gathered her things and made her way to the edge of town and the agreed upon meeting point. Her heart was beating a mile a minute, not because of the physical exertion of walking, but from fear. She was afraid that someone would try to stop her leaving, because in fact, she had absolutely no intention of returning home. She had told her parents that this trip would be no more than a week, but really, once she reached freedom, she would not be returning. They would all have to deal with the fact that this would be the end of her time in the community. She was moving on, starting today.

Just as she smiled to herself with that thought, she heard a rhythmic screeching sound growing louder and louder. She put her bags on the ground and looked down the road. To her astonishment she saw that the sound was coming from an approaching car. The paint was a dull black color, as if they sun and years of use had faded the bright sheen she had often seen on the cars of the English when they were out on the road. There were large rust patch near the rear wheel on her side. There were a smattering of different size dents and scratches on the body of the car. And one window had a large sheet of plastic taped over it, as if the glass must be missing. And just as the car reached her, it stopped. She held her breath as out climbed Phillip. This must have been his cousin's car. His bright smile made her insides warm, but then a sinking feeling crept into the pit of her stomach as they greeted each other. This was not what she had expected, and she was just praying that the rest of what she would encounter would be less shockingly disappointing.

She smiled in spite of her doubts and climbed into the very first car that she had ever ridden in. "Phillip, this is quite an automobile," she said pleasantly, trying to feel out how he felt about the situation.

"It's a piece of junk. It's on its last leg. My cousin had to sell his old car that I thought he had because he needed money. He bought this one for what he could afford. I told him that he overpaid." Phillip laughed jovially and placed his hand on her knee in an affectionate way. It seemed that he was taking the car situation in stride, so she would try to do the same. After all, she had lived her whole life without a car, she could do it still.

"It would seem so." She laughed along with him, but still had trouble shaking the feeling that things were not going to be how she had been hoping.

However, when they arrived at their destination, she found herself cautiously optimistic. They parked in a lot next to a building that seemed to have multiple entrances.

"We are up on the third floor. We climb those outside stairs and then we enter up there under that small roof."

Ruby looked up and squinted against the sun to see the door to which Phillip had been referring. It was at the top of three very long flights of old wooden steps. "Are those stairs safe?"

"Oh sure," he said. "We go up and down all the time. They're sturdier than they look. " But then on an afterthought he added, "But please do hold onto the railing."

They ascended the stairs together with her bags, and by the time they got to the top, Ruby was slightly dizzy from the exertion and the height. They entered together and stepped inside. Ruby stood for a moment allowing her eyes to adjust to the relative darkness inside. The shades were drawn against the sun and there was a television set flickering against the darkness. The room was sparsely furnished with a couch, a number of large cushions that seemed to act as floor cushions, the television on a brown bookshelf, and a number of boxes stacked in the corner. It appeared clean though, and smelled as if someone had recently used a lemon-scented soap.

A young man dressed in English clothing, a couple of years older than them, sat on a worn brown couch staring at the TV and eating something crunchy from a bag. When he saw her, she smiled and stood, brushing his hand off on his blue jeans. "You must be Ruby. Welcome to chaos." He let out a hearty laugh and pointed at Phillip. "I'm this guy's cousin, Robert, though no one else in the family admits that I even exist." He laughed again.

Phillip shook his head at Robert's words. "Well, if it bothers you, you could always come back and apologize for your misguided decisions." His tone was light and teasing, but hinted at their shared history, which was likely unpleasant if he was no longer talking to any of the family.

"Not in a million years, cousin. I got out and I'm not interested in going back." There was something dark lingering below the jovial exterior that Robert put out. It seemed to Ruby that he was bitter. Being excommunicated for making a choice that you are within your rights to make was an unfair reality that they would all be facing. But, in her opinion it was easier than spending the rest of your life explaining yourself. She suddenly wondered what it was going to feel like when her parents no longer spoke to her. Would she miss them? Would it be scary? No, this was something that she had wanted for too long to just give in to doubts and fears now!

As the men told her about where she would be sleeping and how the arrangements would work for rent and other logistical matters, a beautiful woman with long, jean-clad legs strode down the hall. She wore a white sweater that hugged her curvaceous figure. Her hair was brown and wavy as it fell loosely around her smiling face and bright eyes. It took Ruby a moment to realize who she was looking at. When she did, a jolt of surprised rushed through her. "Annabelle?!"

"Hey, Ruby!" Annabelle's smile was wide and her eyes were sparkling. Ruby had never seen her friend to happy.

"You look so different," was all that Ruby managed to get out.

"She looks incredible," said Robert, as he reached for Annabelle's hip and pulled her to him. She let out a throaty chuckle and leaned into him. The moment was so intimate Ruby had to fight to not look away.

"Annabelle has taken to the English lifestyle more quickly than we have," said a teasing voice from the hallway. Donna entered the room in her Amish dress, her brown hair falling loosely around her face.

Ruby looked at her friend. Her hair was beautiful, but her face was not as happy as Annabelle's. And she was surprised to see that Donna was the one not fully embracing the lifestyle available to them.

"Well, now that you're here, I am going to head out to work."

Ruby whipped her head around. "Work?!"

"Yep, he said with a grin, any of us that are staying here longer than two weeks are expected to get jobs to help pay the rent and part of the food bill. "I'm doing some yard work for some of the families in the neighborhood. No worries, Ruby, we'll get you all settled in before you need to go to work." He laughed and waved them off as he walked out the front door.

Annabelle and Robert were now seated, limbs entwined on that couch, completely ignoring the television and the other two human beings in the room. "Come on, Ruby, let's get you settled. You and I will be sharing a room."

As they walked down the hall together, she saw that it was a three bedroom apartment. "Where does Annabelle sleep if Robert and Phillip both have a room?"

"She stays with Robert." Donna kept walking, pretending to ignore the impact that her words had made.

"Oh," was all that Ruby could think to say. She was shocked. She wanted freedom, but this went against everything that they had been taught their whole lives. And for Annabelle to be the one to go down that road, it was as unexpected as the piece-of-junk car that Phillip had pulled up in. Ruby always thought that she would be the one to test the limits, and it was humbling to realize that her boundaries were not as pliable as she had once believed.

"In here," said Donna with a small shake of her head. "Ruby you're going to need to get used to all of this pretty quickly if you plan on having any fun here."

"Oh, right, I know," she said with bravado that she didn't really feel. "So how in the world did that happen? You all only left a handful of weeks ago and she was as timid as a kitten when she left."

"You wouldn't believe it, Ruby. The first few days we were here she kept to herself and sort of just took everything in with wide eyes. We talked about needing to find jobs and what it would be like to meet new people. Robert had been through all of this only a couple of years ago. When he decided to leave the community, his family cut him off and he had to learn how to live all on his own. He was giving us great advice and helping us get acclimated. Then one day he said that he was going to bring us to a party, and out of nowhere, Annabelle said she wanted to dress like him, like a 'regular' person. I don't know where that came from. It was mean and Annabelle has never been mean. She'd been out looking for work and I wonder if someone had said something to her. But, anyway, Robert was happy to indulge her and found out that under her dress she is what he calls a 'knock-out.' It happened that night between the two of them and they have been inseparable ever since. She's changed so much so quickly."

"Well, what does her family think?"

"That's the craziest part, Ruby. She told her family that she won't be baptized into the community and will not be returning. She's renounced everything and is staying with Robert!"

Ruby couldn't believe what she was hearing. Annabelle was always the one that had assumed that her time away would be a chance to see a little of the world before she fully embraced her fate and her role in the Amish community. The fact that there was no whisper of that innocent girl in the woman outside the door scared Ruby more than she cared to admit.

"What did they do to her?" she said without thinking.

Donna's look was dark as she wound her hair tightly into a bun under her own bonnet. "I don't know Ruby, but I don't want it to happen to me. This is going to be my last weekend here. I'm going to go home. I just wanted to wait for you, but I can't stay here. It is too crazy here. I don't want any of this.

Ruby was thrown for yet another loop. Donna had always been so strong, fearlessly adjusting to what was happening in her life. This was not the same girl that had left her only weeks ago.

"Donna, what happened?" She stepped into Donna's space and forced eye contact. "Where is my fearless, happy-go-lucky friend?"

"I just don't like it here, Ruby. I don't understand the way the people are. Everything is much faster and harder. Our lives at home aren't easy all the time, but at least I understand my role and my place. I'm going to be leaving and heading home Monday morning. I'm ready to commit to a baptism and a life there."

"Donna, that's too fast. You know we can take all the time we want. Are you sure this isn't just a rough adjustment?"

Donna's face was suddenly angry. "Just because you hate how we were brought up doesn't mean that I have to. I don't like it here. The men are different. The women are different. The expectations are way different. I just want to go home." Her eyes were welling with tears.

Ruby threw her arms around her friend and rubbed her back. "Okay. I'm sorry." She could count on one hand the number of time she had seen her friend cry. Suddenly she didn't care about finding out what had happened, she just wanted her friend to be happy, and that meant she would be leaving the day after tomorrow.

Suddenly there was a loud pounding from the living room. It sounded as if someone was banging down the front door. The pounding stopped and a raised voice carried down the hallway to the women.

"You have until Monday, Robert. That's it!"

"Can't I just have until the end of the month?" Robert's voice sounded desperate as he answered at a lower volume.

"No. I've giving you enough extensions. I know you have your freaky Amish friends in and out of here all the time. If you can't afford the rent, get a smaller place and stop bringing in all these weird ass roommates that only last weeks or months at a time."

"What about Friday?"

"Wednesday. No later. I mean it, Robert. Forget legal action. I'll have your crap thrown out onto the sidewalk!" There was a loud slamming of the door and then a murmur of voices as Annabelle and Robert spoke words the women could not hear.

They sat quietly for a moment and then looked up when Annabelle poked her head around the door. Clean up, girls, we're meeting Phillip at work and heading to a party.

* * *

They arrived at a house party right down the street from Robert's building long after the sun had set. Annabelle and Robert led the way. Ruby followed and Robert stayed protectively behind her. Donna had decided to stay home, saying that she wasn't feeling up to going anywhere. There was a rhythmic base sound shaking the building and strobe lights flashes through the downstairs windows. Cups littered the front lawn and couples were wrapped around each other in a ways that were considered indecent back home. Sure, they had their own strange courtship rituals, but nothing as open as this.

Ruby had opted to borrow some of Annabelle's English clothing to get the full effect of the evening, but she had left her bonnet on, unable to part with everything about home. She had grabbed the loosest jeans and most discrete top that Annabelle owned, but her curves were still more on display than she had ever experienced. She was amazed that just a couple of months ago she had longed to wear a bikini in public.

Annabelle and Robert immediately headed off into the kitchen to meet-up with some of his friends. Robert was speaking to a group of men that he must have met since moving to the apartment because she didn't recognize any of them as being Amish. And she was left to wonder alone, exploring the party.

Ruby knew that she was considered attractive enough in her community. Her features were delicate, but her body and will were strong. She was curvaceous in a healthy way, and she wore her Amish clothing well. While she had seen men looking at her subtly, she had never experienced the kind of attention that found her that evening. Men were outright touching her, making sexual comments toward her.

One man came up to her and stood blocking her path. "Excuse me," she said, as forcefully as possible through the growing panic. She had never seen anyone behave so aggressively toward a woman before.

He didn't move. "So, you're one of those Amish chicks, huh?" He said. Some friends around them laughed.

"Please move out of my way."

"Hey now, that's no way to be polite. Maybe they don't teach you that on your freak farms in God's country, baby. But here," her reached out and grabbed a hold of her chin, "we answer direct questions."

"Yes, I'm Amish. Now, please let me through."

"You know what I've heard about Amish girls? I hear they like to party and give absolutely excellent ... oof." The man had stopped mid comment and let out of puff of air as someone grabbed him and threw him into the table behind him.

Phillip stood between the man and Ruby, breathing hard. "She asked you to move, asshole," he growled angrily. "You do not touch her, ever!"

"Screw you, freak. She's ripe and I just wanted a piece." With that, Phillip hauled back and punched the man so hard his head bounced off the table.

"Come on, Ruby. We're leaving now." Phillip was so forceful. She'd never seen him behave like that before. He grabbed her hand and started walking her toward the door.

"What about Annabelle?"

"She's with Robert. She's fine. Besides, she likes these insane parties."

He was practically dragging her with him. As they got further from the noise of the house she pulled hard against him and forced him to stop. "Why are you so angry, Phillip?"

"Are you kidding me, Ruby?" He was yelling at her now. "He was touching you. He was trying to take advantage of you. And if you hadn't let him, he was going to hurt you. Didn't you see what was happening there?"

"Of course I did, but if I'm going to live here, I'm going to have to get used to it, right?"

"No way. You are not going to have to get used to it. Even here that behavior is not okay." He started pacing around. "See, this is what scares me so much about you being here. You don't think."

"Excuse me? I do so think."

"No you don't. You have some singular goal to escape home, and you'll walk into anything to reach that goal, even a crap life like this. Why do you need to leave us to be happy? Why do you need to leave me?"

She was suddenly speechless.

"Ruby, you have to know how much your leaving would hurt me. Don't you even realize what you are to me, to all of us? Annabelle is lost to us, seduced by what she sees as a glamorous lifestyle, but you're too smart for that."

"Phillip, I really don't understand why you're so upset. You've known I wanted to live out from under my parents thumb for years."

"There are other ways of doing that, Ruby! You don't have to run away."

"Oh yeah? Name one!"

And before she knew what was happening, he lunged forward and kissed her. At first it was desperate, but then it turned soft. She felt fire blaze through every inch of her body as he wrapped his arms around her when she went weak at the knees. He pulled away and looked at her. "That's my suggestion. Come home with me. Be with me. Ruby, I need you. I only came here so that I could be here for you when you tried to escape. Don't think, my stubborn girl, that I didn't know that you had no plans of returning home after this week."

"But you never said anything, Phillip." She felt muddled.

"I wanted you to realize on your own. But my time ran out. You were running. I can't let you go, Ruby. Do you really want to live out here, alone, scraping by like Robert? He doesn't have freedom. He is a slave to work and toil to keep a meager lifestyle because he doesn't have any friends to help him. Maybe Annabelle will turn it around for him. I don't know. But we don't have to share his fate. Come home with me. We can find freedom there, together."

Ruby looked into the passionate eyes of her friend that she had always loved and felt an attraction that she hadn't expected. She saw a future in his eyes, and it was one that included a life of faith with her family. Could it really work, though? She took a deep breath and decided that she really just needed to go with her gut. Nothing that she had seen since she arrived had been more attractive to her than the promise of what she and Phillip could have.

"Well, then, let's go home and tell Donna that we all leave together to go home on Monday morning," she said with a smile.

He wrapped his arms around her and held her for a long moment. "You won't regret this, darling."

She sighed as she melted into him. "I know I won't."

One Amish Summer

SAMANTHA COLLIER

One Amish Summer

The wide plains of Pennsylvania were like undulating waves, tossing over Delilah. She had never seen the sea, but she imagined that it must be like this: never ending, eternal. She felt alone, in the vast landscape.

They had been travelling for a few hours, and she was starting to despair. When would they arrive in at their destination? She had never travelled so far, and for so long. Any trips that her family had made over the years she had been exempt from, because of her health. Her mother had always said that she simply wasn't up to long trips. And so, Delilah had always been left behind, in the care of relatives.

Until now. Now, she was going to stay with her aunt, over the summer period. And all by herself. Her father was taking her there, but he would return home almost immediately.

The buggy jolted over the unfamiliar terrain. Her father frowned, righting the carriage. He wasn't used to this area of the country, either. And she knew that he was doing it under sufferance, at her mother's insistence. He had work to do; he didn't want to take time out of his schedule for this trip. As always, Delilah felt herself a burden.

She didn't even know why her mother had insisted so vehemently. She would have been happier staying at home; she had never sought this out. Yes, it would be nice to catch up with her Aunt Mildred and her cousin Katura, but she had never been with them for long periods of time. She didn't know what to expect.

Delilah had been thrust out of the comfortable bubble that she had lived in all of her life, and she was apprehensive.

At last. Her father turned down a dirt track, and Delilah could see the farmhouse in the distance. As they approached closer, she saw two figures in long blue dresses and crisp white aprons on the front veranda, waiting for them.

"Whoa." Her father drew in the reins, causing the horses to stop sharply. And then, the two figures were running down the steps to greet them.

"You made it!" Aunt Mildred was upon them. Delilah noticed her familiar lopsided smile, and also that her aunt looked older. Her hair had gone almost completely grey. Well, it had been five years since they had last seen each other.

By her side was Delilah's cousin, Katura. Delilah drew in her breath, sharply, when she observed her cousin. In the five years since she had seen her, Katura had grown from a lanky teenager into a well-rounded, confident looking woman. Her smile was bright, and everything about her – her stance, her mannerisms – spoke volumes. Katura knew her place in the world, and her value.

Delilah immediately felt insecure, even more so than usual. How must she appear to them? Had she changed, as well? But she knew, in her heart, that she hadn't blossomed in the same way that her cousin had. She was still the frail, sickly looking girl she had always been.

"Come in, come in," her aunt was saying now. "Welcome!"

Greetings exchanged, they all made their way into the farmhouse. Delilah looked around, entranced. She had never been here before. For the first time, she allowed a tiny stab of excitement enter her heart at the prospect of staying the summer here.

"How was your trip?" Aunt Mildred was bustling around, serving them coffee and cakes.

"Tolerable," her father answered. "We took the back roads where we could, but we couldn't avoid some major ones. The traffic was fierce in some spots." He smiled, a bit wearily. Again, Delilah felt guilty. It was a familiar feeling; she was always demanding attention from her parents, even though she never sought it.

"Well, you are here safely," her aunt answered. "That is all that matters." She turned to her niece, her eyes quietly assessing her. "It is so lovely to see you again, Delilah. We are delighted to have you for the summer."

"Thank you, Auntie," Delilah answered, dismayed as always by how soft her voice was. Why couldn't she be louder, more assertive? "I am pleased to be here. I am looking forward to the visit."

Aunt Mildred smiled. "You will have a great time, I am sure," she said. "Katura will take you under her wing, show you about the district. You have much planned, don't you, Katura?"

Her cousin smiled, but it didn't reach her eyes. "Of course, Mamm," she said, in a bored voice. She didn't once glance at Delilah. "Depending on how well Delilah feels, of course."

This was how it had always been. Everyone always had to make allowances for her health. No wonder Katura already looked burdened with it. She probably had her own plans for the summer, and now she had to mind her sickly cousin.

"How is your health, Delilah?" Aunt Mildred asked. "Have you improved at all?"

"Much, thank you, Aunt," Delilah answered, casting anxious eyes towards her cousin. "I can't do any vigorous physical activities, but I can go for short walks, longer than before." She turned to Katura. "I will try to keep up with you, cousin."

Katura snorted. "So no swimming or camping, then?" she said. Her eyes looked disdainful. "My friends and I were planning a trip next week, but I suppose I must decline." She sighed, a tad dramatically.

There was an awkward silence at the table. Delilah felt her heart plummet in her chest. This was not a good start to the visit. Her cousin already resented her for being there.

"I am sure there will be lots that Delilah can do," Aunt Mildred nodded her head, decisively. "We will just have to think it through." Almost as an afterthought she turned to her niece. "You are most welcome here, Delilah." Then her eyes turned to her own daughter. Waves of disapproval emanated from her. "Katura is also very glad to have you here."

"Very glad," echoed Katura. Delilah wasn't fooled; her cousin wouldn't even look at her.

Delilah felt the familiar dread. She had made a mistake. She should never have let her mother talk her into this trip. She had spoilt everyone's summer.

But it was all too late, now.

***

Her father had left, declining the offer for lunch. "I must get back," he had said. He turned to Delilah, taking her hands in his. "I hope you have a wonderful time, daughter." Then he had put his black hat on his head and departed.

She was shown to the room that she would stay in, up the stairs, opposite Katura's. It was a good sized room, with a wrought iron single bed covered by a colourful quilt. The window showed a view out to the valley, and beyond.

As she unpacked, she lamented her weakly constitution. It had always got in the way.

She remembered when it had happened. Before that, she had been the same as every other child, able to climb and run outside. She had been boisterous, and happy.

It had been a bitterly cold winter, the year that she had turned eight. So cold; Delilah could still remember shivering in her bed, despite layers of quilts. A virus had spread through the district, felling almost everyone in its path. It particularly struck the weak; old people with little immunity were keeling over from it.

When it had entered their house, she had been struck the worst. A very bad influenza, that racked her body. Her mother had tended her almost around the clock. And then, it had gotten worse. Pneumonia.

She could still remember how panicked she had felt, that she was unable to draw breath. She had felt that was drowning in the fluids in her lungs. And the fever! Half the time she had been delirious, not knowing where she was. She remembered her mother and father standing at the doorway to her room, their brows knotted with worry.

She had recovered, slowly. But the pneumonia had left its mark. It had scarred her lungs, and she simply was never the same again. She could no longer climb and run, as she once had. Most of the time, she stayed in the living room, a rug over her knees. She became known as delicate; the friends that she had once had no longer came to play. Her own brothers and sisters would run off outside, and they never asked her to join them, anymore. Even if they had, her mother wouldn't have allowed it.

Delilah frowned, remembering. Had her mother been over protective? Could she have done more, or at least, been encouraged to? She knew that her parents worried about her, so much. She thought now that they had probably wrapped her in cotton wool. Which was why she had never been on any long trips, before.

"Are you unpacked?"

Delilah glanced up from what she was doing. It was Katura.

"*Jah*, all done," she answered, looking at her cousin. "I am sorry, Katura. I don't want to be a burden."

Katura's gaze softened slightly. "Don't be silly," she sniffed. "Can you sing? After service tomorrow, the Evening Sing is happening. I'd like you to come. There's a young man I've got my eye on."

"Really?" Delilah smiled. "What is his name?"

"Isaiah King," Katura breathed. "He is wonderful! I think that he is going to ask me to court, soon."

Katura sat down on the bed, and regaled Delilah with everything about this Isaiah: his manners, his history, and his appearance. Judging by her cousin's shining eyes, Delilah could tell that Katura was serious about him.

She listened and nodded, but all the while felt sadness. It was ridiculous. She should be happy for her cousin. But self-pity overwhelmed Delilah.

She would never be courted, or asked to marry. She would never have a family or a home of her own, despite what her mother thought. Delilah knew that one reason her mother had insisted on this trip was in the vain hope that Delilah might meet somebody. No young man in her own district ever paid her a shred of attention, and why should they? She was known as sickly. She couldn't do the things that everyone else could. What man would want a semi invalid for a wife? They wanted strong, vibrant girls who could work alongside them.

If she were honest, Delilah knew that her mother had half created the situation, by being so over protective. Maybe Delilah could have done more, or been pushed to at least try.

No, love wasn't for her. Love was for girls like Katura, who shone with energy and life. Delilah was destined to be a spinster, forever sitting in her parents' home, wasting away year after year.

She shouldn't resent her cousin. It was unkind; God wouldn't like it. He didn't look kindly on girls who felt sorry for themselves. Acceptance, Delilah thought. I must accept my lot in life, and not dream of anything more.

With her resolve in place, Delilah turned to her cousin, and let herself truly feel excited for her.

"I can't wait to meet Isaiah," she told her.

***

Delilah glanced around the unfamiliar barn, and the unfamiliar faces singing to heaven. Her heart was pounding, painfully. She wasn't used to being in crowds, and certainly not amongst unfamiliar people. The only person she knew at this Evening Sing was Katura, and of course her cousin knew everybody.

Her cousin nudged her, staring over at a young man further down. Judging by her cousin's shining eyes, the young man was him. Isaiah King. The one that Katura was sure was about to ask her to start courting.

Delilah studied him. He was indeed handsome, and his eyes shone with kindness. She felt a stirring, an unfamiliar feeling entering her soul. She frowned – what was she thinking? Her cousin was sweet on this man. Delilah shook her head, trying to dislodge the feeling.

And yet it stayed with her, all through the hymns. A sweet, yearning feeling that she had simply never felt before.

The hymns over, everyone got up. Katura took Delilah's arm, leading her over to Isaiah.

"Isaiah," her cousin breathed. He turned around, looking at them both.

His eyes widened as he looked at Delilah. She felt herself blushing; it seemed to take over her, feeling much like a fever.

"This is my cousin, Delilah," Katura said. "She is staying with us for the summer."

The young man held out his hand. "Greetings, Delilah. Welcome to our district."

She took his hand, shaking it. Did he hang onto it just a tad too long? He was certainly staring at her. Delilah glanced nervously at Katura. Her cousin was frowning.

Delilah broke the contact abruptly. "Thank you," she said, awkwardly.

Another young man had come over to them, looking at them expectantly. Delilah turned to look at him. His eyes were cold, and he wasn't smiling.

"Isaiah, we must away," the other young man said. "You know how early a start we have tomorrow."

Isaiah sighed. "Of course," he said. "But you must meet the young lady who is visiting us for the summer. Delilah, this is my brother, Jeremiah."

Jeremiah barely glanced at her. He was frowning. "*Jah*, nice to meet you," he said. He turned back to Isaiah. He looked like he couldn't wait a minute longer.

"Well, I'm sure we will see each other again," Isaiah said to her. He looked at her one last time, then seemed to remember that Katura was standing there, looking at him. "Katura, are you coming swimming with us, over at the lake next week?"

"I would," Katura answered. "But Delilah can't swim, and my mother insists that I don't do anything without her." Was there a little eye roll as she spoke? Delilah's face burned again.

"But Delilah must come," Isaiah smiled. "Of course you must."

"Oh, I have never learnt to swim..." Her voice trailed off. How pathetic must she sound?

"You can still enjoy the day, can't you?" He smiled. "Even if you can't swim, you can sit and be in nature, surely?"

"Well..." Delilah looked at Katura, a bit desperately. How should she respond?

"It's settled, then." Isaiah put his hat on his head. "I will pick both of you up this Thursday."

"Isaiah." Jeremiah was impatiently looking toward the door.

"Coming." With a last glance back at the girls, Isaiah left with his brother.

Katura sighed, deeply. "See, what a wonderful man he is?" she said to her cousin. "Including you, just because of me! You must come, Delilah. As Isaiah said, you can watch."

Delilah nodded, slowly. She didn't seem to have much choice. And she had wanted to join in, hadn't she? She had dreamed of being able to participate, and be included.

And then, there was the thought of seeing Isaiah again. Her heart started to beat slowly at the thought.

What was wrong with her? Her cousin liked him. She would pray, that God would stop this feeling. It felt wrong. Even though she knew it hardly mattered – it wasn't as if Isaiah would ever consider her in that way, even if he had no interest at all in Katura.

***

"Isaiah! Stop splashing!"

Delilah watched from the bank, as the group of young people splashed in the water. Oh, how she longed to be able to join in! The water looked so inviting, especially on this hot day. She was sweating.

Katura was laughing, enjoying herself. Delilah watched her look at Isaiah from beneath her eyelashes, making every excuse to be near him. Delilah didn't think that Isaiah looked at Katura in any special way; he was equally friendly with everybody. Had her cousin misread his regard for her?

She watched his brother, Jeremiah, off by himself. He didn't seem to want to join in with the others. He gazed over the lake, seemingly deep in thought. He didn't look happy. Delilah felt a dark wave go over her. Why didn't she like him? There was just a feeling she got. As much as she had felt a glow when she had first met Isaiah, she felt a darkness around Jeremiah.

She had always been intuitive about people. It was like she could read them, straight away. Maybe it was her spells of illness; it had heightened her senses, in some way. She had always been an observer of life, rather than a participant.

The swimmers waded out now, laughing. But Jeremiah stayed by himself in the water, a dark cloud hanging over his head.

Isaiah looked at Delilah. "Are you enjoying yourself?" he asked her, smiling. "It is such a beautiful day." His eyes locked into hers. Delilah didn't think that she had ever seen such blue eyes before. They seemed to sear into her soul, touching her inside.

"Delilah," he said, seeming at a loss of words. He looked over his shoulder at Katura, who had wondered along the bank with some other people. "I was wondering whether you might like to accompany me to a restaurant in town, next week?" He looked down, blushing.

Delilah's breath caught in her throat. "With Katura, you mean?"

"*Nein*," he shook his head, gazing at her again. "I mean, just you and I."

Was he asking her to court? Delilah couldn't believe it; had she imagined the words? She stared at him, dumbfounded.

"But...but..." she stammered. "Don't you like Katura? She likes you."

Isaiah looked back at Katura. "I know she does," he sighed. "But I like her just as a friend." He gazed at her, intently. "The minute I saw you, Delilah, I knew. That we had a connection. Can you deny it?"

She shook her head, slowly. She had felt it, too, instantly, but she had dismissed it. She wasn't used to it, and besides, Katura liked him.

"I just don't know," she whispered. She could see Katura looking over at them, frowning. Oh dear Lord, what was she doing?

"Think about it," Isaiah said. "There isn't anything between Katura and I, despite what she may wish. There would be no betrayal of her, if that is what makes you hesitate."

"I will think about it," Delilah whispered.

Isaiah smiled. "Jeremiah, Samuel and I are going to do a spot of fishing, now," he said. "Maybe you can tell me your decision when we all meet up, again."

Delilah watched Jeremiah leave the water, staring over at his brother. The other young man, Samuel, had already picked up their fishing rods. "Are you ready, Isaiah?" he called.

"Coming," he called back. He smiled at Delilah, then joined the others. They walked off, into the woods.

"What was Isaiah talking to you about?"

Delilah started. Katura was looming over her. And she didn't look happy.

***

Delilah wondered later, after the events of the day had unfolded, how everything changed in a heartbeat.

Katura had pressed her for details about Isaiah, but Delilah had said that he merely was chatting with her. She knew that she should have told her cousin that Isaiah had asked her out, but she couldn't bring herself to.

They had both sat there, in stony silence, when they heard it.

The scream. A bloodcurdling scream, which seemed to echo around the woods.

Delilah and Katura jumped to their feet, looking at each other fearfully. "What was that?" Katura said. "Is it the men?"

Katura ran off, and Delilah jumped to her feet, following. She couldn't run as fast as the other girl; even now, her breath came in painful rasps. The woods seemed impenetrable. What had happened?

Eventually, she got to where Katura was, standing still. And she saw everything.

Isaiah and Jeremiah, standing there. But Samuel was on the ground, seemingly out cold. The two brothers looked down at him. They both looked like they were in shock.

Delilah didn't think. She simply rushed over to the prone man, crouching over him. His eyes weren't open. And there was a deep gash on his forehead, oozing blood.

"What happened?" Delilah ripped her apron, pressing the material against the head wound, trying desperately to stem the bleeding.

The brothers stood there, looking down. Neither of them spoke.

"Katura," she called. "Can you help?"

Her cousin seemed to come to her senses, rushing over to them. "Dear Lord, is he alive?"

Delilah pressed her face against his chest. "Just barely."

She turned to the two men. "You have to pick him up!" she shouted. "Why are you both standing there? We have to get him to hospital, as quickly as possible."

The two men came over, the spell broken. "*Jah*, of course," said Jeremiah. He picked up Samuel's legs. Isaiah slowly walked around to his head.

"Oh, God," he suddenly cried. His face was ashen. "This is my fault. I did this."

Delilah's heart went cold.

***

It was all like a dream, afterwards. The trip to the hospital. Desperately trying to stem Samuel's bleeding. The questions, none of which she could answer.

And then, as they all sat in the hospital ward, waiting for news about Samuel's condition, the police had arrived.

They had questioned them all, separately.

Delilah had left the room, to get herself a drink of water. She was shaking from delayed shock. The nurses had told her that she had done the right thing, trying to stop the bleeding. She had probably saved Samuel's life, but he wasn't good. He was in a coma, and she could tell by the rushing around, the whispers and frowns, that it might still happen. He might die.

Then the police had taken Isaiah away. Delilah still couldn't believe it. How could he be responsible for this? She didn't know him well, but her instincts had never been wrong about people before. He was a good man, she knew it.

And then, it hit her: she was falling in love with him. She had never thought that it could happen so quickly. She had heard about love at first sight, but always dismissed it as fiction. But it was true: it had happened to her.

And now, she watched helplessly as her new love was dragged away, seemingly about to be charged for this evil act.

She turned to look at Jeremiah. How was he feeling – it was his brother, after all, that had just been taken away by the police.

But Jeremiah sat there, a stony look on his face. A nerve twitched in his brow, but he said nothing. Nothing.

Katura was pale. "Delilah, we should leave," she whispered. "My mother will be worried, we are so late. There is nothing more that we can do here."

Delilah nodded. But she watched Jeremiah as they left, sitting there like a statue. She could almost see the dark cloud over his head.

There was more to this. She just knew it.

***

That night, she and Katura stayed up late, drinking cocoa and trying to make sense of the strange and troubling events of the day.

"I simply can't believe it," Katura whispered, shaking her head. "It is so out of character. I went to school with Isaiah, and I have never once seen any anger or tendency to violence in him. Not once!"

Delilah sipped her cocoa, frowning. "Tell me about Jeremiah. What is he like?"

Katura shuddered. "I have never liked him," she said. "Furtive. Always watching, but not in a good way."

"Have you ever seen him act in a violent manner?"

"No, I don't think so." Katura frowned, thinking. "He is not hot headed. At school, he was always behind the scenes if there were any altercations. I always got the sense that he might be egging things on, but he would never act himself."

Delilah frowned, thinking it through. It was a mystery.

The fact that Isaiah had asked her out, just prior to the incident occurring. He had seemed carefree, happy. What had gone on between the three men, to change everything so drastically? They had set out to fish. It had been a beautiful day.

A vision of Jeremiah in the water came to her. Frowning. Separate.

"And what about Samuel, Katura?" she asked her cousin. "Is he close to both?"

"Samuel is Isaiah's best friend," answered Katura. "They have been inseparable since they were little." She pressed a hand to her forehead. "I cannot think about it anymore. I must go to bed. Will you retire also?"

Delilah smiled faintly at her cousin. "In a moment. I will finish my drink. Good night, dear cousin."

She reached out and took Katura's hand. Her cousin looked surprised, but squeezed it. Then she drifted up the stairs to bed.

Delilah felt so tired she could almost have put her head on the table and slept there. She should go to bed, but her mind was whirring so much she knew that sleep would elude her.

The sudden, world shifting attraction between Isaiah and herself. Then the incident, that Isaiah had taken responsibility for. She still didn't know what had happened; both men refused to speak. Had Isaiah pushed Samuel because of a sudden disagreement, and he had hit his head? Or had the act been more deliberate? But Samuel was his best friend. And Isaiah didn't have that darkness in him; she was sure of it.

And then there was the fact that Jeremiah had said nothing. Not even when the police had taken his brother away.

Was Isaiah covering up for Jeremiah? But, why would he?

Delilah looked at the clock. It was about to chime midnight. There would be no answers tonight. She would think about it tomorrow, with a clear head.

She drifted up the stairs to bed, worry eating at her soul.

***

She tossed and turned all night. When she was asleep, strange, vivid dreams took hold of her.

They were back at the lake. Jeremiah was in the water, way into the distance. She was watching him, her breath getting shallower. Suddenly, she was in the water herself, desperately trying to swim.

"Help me," she cried out. Jeremiah watched her, his face impassive. She knew he had heard her, but he didn't move.

Then, Isaiah was there. "Don't worry," he whispered. "I will save you." Samuel was by his side, nodding. "Trust him, Delilah," he said. "He won't let you down."

She woke up, suddenly. She was indeed gasping for breath. She sat up, and reached over for the glass of water on the bedside table. Her hand was shaking.

Isaiah wasn't guilty. She knew it, now. He could never do such a thing.

But Jeremiah could. She was equally sure of that.

***

Delilah watched Samuel in the hospital bed, hooked up to machines. His eyes were closed; he looked like he was sleeping peacefully. As if his eyelids might flutter suddenly, and he would stretch and awaken.

But it wasn't as simple as that. For Samuel was in a coma, and he mightn't ever awake from it.

And if he didn't, Isaiah would be charged with murder.

Delilah came into the room, resting on her knees beside the bed. She prayed to God, fervently. She prayed that Samuel wouldn't lose his life. He was so young, and had his whole life before him. Delilah didn't know him at all, but she had liked him. She also prayed for Isaiah. She still simply could not believe that he had done this. She prayed that the truth of what had happened would be revealed.

She picked up Samuel's hand. His family had left the room, just five minutes prior. She still felt the awful grief and horror that had been left in their wake. His mother had looked devastated, as if her world had collapsed. And his father had been tight lipped with grief.

"Samuel." She whispered, stroking his hand. "I know I don't know you well. Please wake up. Your family need you. Wake up, Samuel, and tell people what really happened to you. We need to know."

She watched his face, but there wasn't a flicker. The only sound in the room was the beeping of the machines.

Delilah sighed, feeling as low as she had ever felt. She loved Isaiah. Why was he claiming that he had done this? She knew in her heart it simply wasn't true.

She must speak with him.

***

Isaiah looked like he had aged a thousand years. Grief etched his features.

Delilah sat opposite him, across the sparse table at the police station.

"How are you?" she whispered.

He sighed, blinking back tears. "Don't ask me," he responded. "I don't deserve it. I deserve nothing."

Delilah closed her eyes for a moment. "Isaiah, I don't believe you. I know that you couldn't have done this to Samuel."

Isaiah just looked at her, sadly. "I am so sorry, Delilah," he sighed. "For everything. For what could have been, between us. I know it is sudden; I know that we hardly know each other. But I was falling in love with you."

Tears slid down Delilah's face. "I am in love with you, Isaiah. I tried to fight it, because of Katura, but it is what it is. Like what is between us existed before we even knew about it." She wiped the tears away. "And that is how I know that you are innocent. I am very intuitive about people; I knew straight away that you were a good soul. But what about Jeremiah?"

Isaiah looked up at her, sharply. But he didn't say a word.

"What about us?" she pressed. "If you take responsibility for this, we will never have a chance. And your life will be over."

"Don't you think I know that?" He looked haggard. "But family is family. And Jeremiah is my little brother."

Delilah looked at him, sharply. There it was. She knew for sure, now.

Jeremiah had done this. And Isaiah had taken the blame, because he was his baby brother, and he wanted to protect him.

Isaiah was willing to give up his own life, to protect his brother. That was the type of man he was. Delilah wanted to shake him, say that Jeremiah didn't deserve this loyalty; that if he hurt Samuel, he needed to take responsibility for it. That Isaiah wasn't helping him. He was just ruining his own life.

But Isaiah had closed down, and wouldn't speak further. "I am so sorry, Delilah," he whispered. "Please, don't come again. Find a man who deserves you. I pray to God that your life will be happy."

He stood up, and left the room. Delilah watched him leave, her heart breaking.

***

Katura sat with her that night, in the living room.

"I know," she said, turning her head to Delilah. "About you and Isaiah. That you have fallen in love with each other."

Delilah gasped. "How did you know?" she asked. Tears streamed down her face, for the second time that day. "I am so sorry, Katura. I never wanted to hurt you."

"It's okay," whispered Katura. "I think I knew, deep down, that Isaiah wasn't interested in me. And he never gave me any indication that there might be a possibility of the two of us courting. It was all just wishful thinking on my part." She breathed out, deeply. "It's alright, Delilah. You both have my blessing."

Delilah leaned over and hugged her cousin. "It doesn't matter, anyway," she whispered. "Isaiah is determined to take the blame for the incident, and he told me that I should move on. That I should find someone else." She sighed, deeply. "But I never will."

"You don't think Isaiah did it?" said Katura. "You think it was Jeremiah?"

"I do," said Delilah. "But he won't admit it. Why is he doing this?"

Katura smiled, grimly. "There is only the two of them," she said. "Their parents died years ago, and they have no one else in the family. They live together, on their property. Isaiah has always looked out for Jeremiah, protected him."

It made sense, then. Isaiah's overarching loyalty to Jeremiah. A loyalty so strong, he was even prepared to take the blame for something that would ruin his life. And Samuel was his best friend, as well.

"We should pray," whispered Delilah. "It is the only thing that we can do."

Both young women closed their eyes. Delilah prayed harder than she had ever in her life.

***

God answered their prayers.

Aunt Mildred told them the good news as soon as they came down for breakfast. "Girls, Samuel Stoltzfus has woken up!" she said, her eyes shining. "The Lord has heard us."

Delilah and Katura embraced, hugging each other tightly. Tears of joy fell down their faces.

"And you know what else?"

They both looked at her, expectantly.

"Samuel has told the police that Jeremiah pushed him," Aunt Mildred continued. "He said they argued, and Jeremiah just lashed out. Samuel must have hit his head on a rock when he fell." Aunt Mildred lifted her eyes to heaven. "Isaiah has been released from custody."

Delilah gasped. All her prayers had been answered. Isaiah was free! And he hadn't done anything to Samuel. She had known, all along!

She started weeping. Aunt Mildred came over to her, looking at her tenderly.

"I think you should go and see him," she whispered. "I will drive you over there myself."

***

He was standing on the front veranda when they pulled up. Delilah could see his eyes light up when he realised it was her.

"I will pick you up later?" asked Aunt Mildred. "Or will you bring her back?"

"I will bring her back," smiled Isaiah. "Thank you."

"I am so glad everything has worked out," Aunt Mildred said. Then she turned and drove off.

They looked at each other shyly. He took her hand, and led her up onto the veranda. They sat down, staring out over the farm.

Delilah kept sneaking glances at him. She simply couldn't believe that he was here, and that everything had worked out, in the end.

Isaiah couldn't stop staring at her, either.

"Where is Jeremiah?" she whispered.

"At the police station," he said. "Giving another statement. I'm sorry, Delilah. I thought I was doing the right thing, protecting him. But I shouldn't have done it." He sighed, deeply. "But it wasn't deliberate. Jeremiah pushed Samuel, but he didn't intend what happened. I know that."

Delilah frowned, thinking of the dark cloud that surrounded Jeremiah, but she kept her thoughts to herself.

"Samuel is going to be fine," she said, instead, focusing on the good news. "Apparently, he is going to make a full recovery."

"Praise the Lord," said Isaiah. He looked like he was going to break down, again. "What about us, Delilah? Will you be willing to marry a man who has been charged with attempted murder?"

Delilah looked at him, filled with love. "No," she said. He looked devastated. She smiled. "Not a man charged with attempted murder. But I would be willing to marry a man who is so loyal to his brother, he will do anything to protect him." She paused. "Even if that loyalty was misguided."

Isaiah stood up, pulling her up with him. "What about Katura? Does she understand?"

"Jah," answered Delilah. "We spoke of it the other night. She is happy for the both of us."

"Then everything is how it should be," Isaiah breathed. "We can start over. What about that date on Saturday night?"

Delilah burst out laughing. "Why not?" she answered.

They walked down the veranda steps, laughing and talking. Delilah reflected that it had certainly been a summer to remember, so far. A crime, a jilted cousin, and a marriage proposal.

What on earth would the rest of the summer bring? She would leave that in the hands of the Lord. He seemed to make everything good, in the end.

THE END

SWEETLY AMISH

MARIAH MOORE

Hope twisted her apron skirt in her hands nervously. She and Rachel had both been courting men lately. Oh, how they had fallen in love. They had agreed to invite the men over for dinner on the same night. As Hope thought of her courting man, she smiled unconsciously. His deep brown eyes, his tanned skin, and his sand-colored hair all indicted a couple of things. One – that he wasn't from this part of the area. Two – he probably got lost the first time she met him.

Their community wasn't easy to find. It required a good hike up what was probably considered a mountain, but most here considered it a rolling hill. Then, one made a hike into the forest on the mountain side. It started about halfway up the side, and the community was about three-quarters of the way up the side.

The point was that it wasn't easy to find. They didn't want to be found.

She softly started to walk around the room. It was getting late, and he hadn't arrived yet. Oddly enough, Rachel's date hadn't arrived yet either. She took a deep breath, trying to stay calm. She didn't need to freak out over the fact that neither of the men had arrived yet.

There was a knock at the door. She pursed her lips. She wasn't sure what to do. Was it Richard, or was it someone else? As the time seemed to tick away from where she was needed it, she found herself walking towards the door.

"Who is it?" She tried to hide her anxiety, her nerves. She took a deep breath, and slowly let it out, trying to hide it from whoever was on the other side of that door.

"Hope, it's me. It's Rachel. Can I come in?" She relaxed a little bit at her sister's voice.

"Yeah. Come on in." She sighed softly. At least this meant that her sister was still single for the night. The door opened, and she moved away to let it swing open and shut softly as it needed to. Rachel walked in, her long hair braided tightly down the back of her neck and to her waist. She had always loved the way Rachel could wear her hair without worrying about what the community would say about it.

Hope typically wore her own hair in two thick braids, one going down each side of her head. She loved the way it looked when it rained – how the rain would sleek the sides and calm the frizz of the jungle's humid air.

"Is your courtier here yet?" She furrowed her brows. Rachel seemed just as upset as she was, and the question wasn't any indication that it would change soon. Hope shook her head.

"Yours?" She frowned. This wasn't going to go anywhere if their dates, for lack of a better word, didn't show up soon. When Rachel shook her head, her frown deepened. This wasn't going to end well for either of them. Their parents were already suspicious of what was going on, but if they didn't show up, this was going to get even worse.

"What are we going to do? They're already skeptical because we're both dating outsiders." Rachel's own frown deepened. Despite being twins, they didn't look alike. Her sister's hair was dark and long. Her own hair was a little shorter, but still just as long and much thicker than her sister's. It wasn't nearly as dark, either.

"I don't know. I wish we had another way to talk to them besides letter or in person, but we don't. Unfortunately." Hope sighed deeply. "What did you say his name was?"

"Richard. Why?" Rachel furrowed her eyebrows, as if she wasn't convinced that there was something wrong yet. "What are you thinking, Hope?" Her sister walked closer to her, but didn't come close enough to touch her.

"What if...what if we have been courting the same person? We haven't met each other's courting matches, and both our dates are late tonight." She tried not to cry, or to let her whirl of emotions show through. "I mean, it's the only thing that really makes sense, isn't it?"

"Are you sure you want to go through that door, Hope?" Her sister, always the skeptic, tried to find a loophole, some shred of doubt. "I really think they're two different people. What's the name of the man you've been courting?"

"Richard." She sighed. Her sister did have a point. The name had been rather common among men lately. Well, men that they had met. How many men had they courted with the name Richard before this point? She had courted at least two others in the community alone.

"See? We've both courted men named Richard before – and this has happened once before. So, let's give them a little more time." Her sister took her into a hug. It was something soft, sweet, and needed. She hugged back softly, trying not to struggle with the idea that they might be unable to find out what was going on.

"Alright." She took a deep, shaky breath. "Let's give them the benefit of the doubt. Is mother done with dinner?" For some reason, their mother had asked that the younger siblings help today, but not her and her sister.

"Yeah. She said that she would call us down when the men arrived. Remember?" Rachel pulled away, still trying to give her sister some shred of something to hold onto. She nodded slowly. "Good. So, let's wait right here."

"Hope, Rachel. They're here." Before Hope could say anything else, their mother poked her head into the door. A soft frown graced her face. Hope simply shot a look over to Rachel. This did not bode well for them. At all. "And I think you have some explaining to do. Come on." She left, leaving the door wide open.

"That wasn't good." Rachel frowned. "Maybe you were right, Hope. But, we won't know until we go down there." She took in a deep breath. Maybe her sister was right. They wouldn't know what was going on until they went downstairs to see what was going on.

So, they walked down the stairs, arm in arm. Rachel stood to the left, while Hope was against the wall to the right. If they were going up, they would have been on the opposite sides – Rachel against the wall and Hope against the railing with the banister. Not that it really mattered to her, anyway. She managed to get all the way down the stairs before both she and Rachel saw the problem.

There was only one man in the room. She recognized him; it was Richard.

"Richard." She looked to Rachel. They'd said his name at exactly the same time. There wasn't much surprise to either of them. Her sister pulled away from her softly. She'd been the one that had been courting more seriously lately out of the two of them. Hope, herself, had some interest in Richard, but she wasn't sure she approved of him anymore. He was courting both of them, but seriously, he could only court one of them.

"Oh. This is awkward." He laughed softly. "Rachel. Hope." He greeted them kindly. He was one for the kind approach, the sweet approach. "I apologize for the confusion, but I did not realize you were sisters when both of you asked me to dinner for the same night. I came to tell you that I had a prior engagement come up that I thought had canceled and I'd have to cut dinner short." He took Rachel's hand first, and kissed it softly. Then, he took her hand and kissed it.

"Did you two realize you were courting the same man?" Their mother smiled a little as he pulled away from Hope. There was a hesitance in his voice, in his face, that made it clear he hadn't realized what was going on.

"No. We did not, mother." Hope spoke first. "But it's alright. Rachel has gone more with him than I have." She laughed a little bit and went to go sit down at the table. "I don't want to cause trouble."

"Hope, it's alright. You don't have to leave." Richard came over to her. "I actually wanted to talk to you. May we talk outside?" He motioned towards the door. She pursed her lips a little. There was something different about the way he approached this one. He wanted her to follow him, but it wasn't in a loving manner. She wondered if something had happened for her to earn his scorn.

"Alright. If you'll excuse us, mother." She nodded her head curtly, and followed him out into the hallway, and then the entryway. He opened the door for her, and they both walked outside onto the porch. The porch itself was a bit of a mosh-posh of her mother's generation and her generation. The couch was old and falling apart. The rockers, on the other hand, were newer. They had been crafted only a couple of years ago.

"I don't mean to be brisk or rude, Hope." Richard sat down on one of the rockers. She sat down on the porch swing, not wanting to make him feel any worse about what he was probably going to do. "I just...I don't feel like we connected as well as I connected with Rachel."

"I figured as much by how few and far between we were together." She put her fingers around the pole that helped the bench swing on its base. Her nails grazed her palm; they probably needed a trim. She frowned a little. "But, why are you beginning here? Why now? Why on my porch?"

"Because I didn't realize how awkward it would be to do it tonight. Hope...I want to stop courting you, or whatever it is you Amish people call it. I just, I don't know how else to tell you that. You don't have the kind of spunk I want in a woman. Rachel does. That's all." He stood up, sighing softly. "Please, don't make this any harder than it has to be."

"It doesn't have to be all that hard if you're only going to take a couple minutes to do it." She stood up again. "I'm sorry that you feel that way, Richard. And, I'm sorry this is going to be a very awkward dinner tonight." She smiled, laughing a little. "But, tell me this. If I don't have what it is you're looking for, what makes you think Rachel has it?"

"There's something different about her that I like. That I don't see in you. Don't get me wrong, you are an amazing woman in your own right, but you have nothing on your sister in this area." He walked over to her, and softly took her hands. "You'll find your own way in the world." He kissed her hand again.

"Thank you, Richard." She took in a deep breath, trying to avoid the lump that was rising in her throat. There was something funny about the way this was going. She wasn't in the mood for this kind of a day, but this was something different. She felt...upset. Disappointed. This wasn't the way she wanted to feel. She didn't want to feel as though this was destroying her life.

"And, I hope that you'll be able to find someone that's right for you." He helped her stand up. There was something even odder about this part. "I think I have fallen in love with your sister, so please, let's not let things got awkward. I think it really could work out between Rachel and me. Please, let me pursue that if I can." He let go of her hand before starting to turn away.

"Richard, I can see the way you look at her." She didn't want to sugarcoat things. "I think you have very much fallen in love with her, but you have no idea how to show that you have. You'll lose her if you don't show her something spectacular." She spoke out of memories, out of experience. Many a man had fallen in love with her sister, and had lost her sister because they didn't know how to show it in a way she understood.

"What do you mean by that, Hope?" He sat back down. Her words seemed to have suddenly intrigued him. "How do you know that?" His brows furrowed in the middle of his forehead.

"I speak from experience, Richard." She sighed softly and sat back down on the swinging bench. "Rachel doesn't like to stay with men that don't show that they appreciate her. She wants a husband, a man, that will do some of the things she routinely does for everyone – you know, give her a break?" She wasn't sure what, exactly, they had been doing for when they had been going out. They would often be out for hours on end.

"I have tried. She seems to approve of it." He smiled softly. "I do not think I'm in any danger of losing her. Of finding our courtship broken over something I never knew about." He laughed a little at this. "Please, do not try to meddle into our relationship just because I broke it off with you. I don't want this to become awkward between us." He pursed his lips.

"Well, it became awkward when Rachel and I were courting the same man. Your pleas not to make it awkward are only making it more awkward for me, Richard. In all honestly, I'd rather you left us both alone now." She got up. "But if you insist on seeing Rachel after you have so rudely broken off our courtship before realizing that you were dating both of us, I want you to know that I will be watching out for her."

Hope walked back towards the door. She had to walk past Richard to do that, and she knew exactly how strong he was. He could easily pull her back and down into the seat beside him if he wanted to continue this conversation. If he wanted to risk her raising her voice.

He didn't pull her aside to continue the conversation. Instead, he got up, and walked in after her.

"Alright." He smiled a little at her, and then dropped the conversation for the rest of the night. However, something else bubbled and roiled inside her. This strange hatred of the affection that he showed Rachel the rest of the night surfaced.

She nibbled at her food. Her mother seemed to notice that something was off, that the air between Richard and herself was cold and harsh now. She didn't make eye contact with him at all the rest of the night, and when he left, she offered him a handshake instead of a hug.

Then, she started to clean up the dinner from that night. The mashed potatoes were put into a large bowl to be stored in the coldest place in the house. There was meat leftover to go out to the pig slough. Most of the leftover vegetables and things would end up out there too.

As she started to gather dishes to clean, she felt a hand on her shoulder.

"I'll do it. You need to go calm down, Hope." It was Rachel's voice. "Richard told me what happened when you went to the porch together. I never meant for this to affect you like this. I'm sorry." She turned to face her sister.

"Rachel, he dumped me because he likes you. There's no shame in that." She managed not to frown deeply at her. "I'm fine. I'll do the dishes; it's my turn anyway. You go to bed." She picked the dishes up again and took them towards the sink. She heard Rachel following her.

"Hope, I was going to call it off with him after that, but he didn't give me a chance to tonight. I plan to call it off soon." She took her sister's hand softly as Hope put the pile on the counter. "Let me at least help you with the dishes, Hope. Please. I don't want this to ruin our sisterhood because of what happened."

"Rachel." She turned to look at her sister. "I don't want this to do it either, but I need to think about what just happened. Please. Leave me alone to do that. I want to think about it doing the dishes, but I want to do it alone." With that, she turned back to the hollowed out sink and the pool of water inside it.

She started to wash a large pot that her mother had used to make the mashed potatoes. As she scrubbed at it, she thought. How could Richard have not realized he was dating twins? While she and Rachel didn't look completely similar, she and her sister looked enough alike that it should have been easy enough to piece together on his own. He shouldn't have needed to wait until they were in the same place to see it.

If he had realized it earlier, he could have broken it off with her without her ever being the wiser about it. Especially since this hadn't been Rachel's idea. This dinner tonight had been Hope's idea. She had wanted an excuse not to climb down the mountain for once.

How it had backfired on her today.

She slammed the rag down on the counter, letting it make a soft thunk-thud as it landed. He wasn't worth the troubling thoughts that she was having. Yet they refused to leave her alone. Maybe being an old, bitter maid would be okay. She wouldn't be mad if that happened to her. He deserved the feeling of regret, of betrayal, that ought to come with breaking off a courtship.

Yet she had given him no reason to feel those things when she had left him on the porch. Unless, of course, by walking away, she had kept him from obtaining the true purpose of what he had come to do. If by walking away, she had given him some reason to suspect that she still loved him, that she still wanted something to do with him, she had managed to give him the remorse, the regret he deserved to feel.

The thought of having done it simply by ending the conversation made her feel better. If she really had given him that remorse, that regret that he deserved, he wouldn't be coming back around here anytime soon.

She picked the rag up from the counter, and continued to scrub away at the pot. There was really very little left on the pot to scrub at, but some of it had burnt on in years past. She was making good progress on getting it up and off the pot. So, using her slightly longer nails, she continued to pick at the burnt-on food.

Picking at the food made her feel even better. Like she had control of something again, as if she were able to pick up and start all over. Eventually, she had to put the pot into the water and actually wash it. With soap bubbles and everything. Her mother wouldn't be happy to know she had spent so much time on one dish.

As she washed the dish, her anger began to fade away. She thought of how she had to move her hands in a circular motion to simply wash the soap over the dish. Once the pot was soaped up and full of soapy water, she dumped the soapy water into the sink.

She continued her routine for a few more minutes before someone else walked into the room. As much as Hope wanted to be alone right now, she didn't want to yell at whoever had walking into the room.

"Are you alright, sweetie?" Her mother's voice entered her ears. She sighed. "Alright. Put the dishes down. What's on your mind?" Her hand trailed up Hope's arm, as if she was waiting for something to happen. As if there was something funny going on about what was happening. She sighed again.

"It's just...this whole thing with Richard. I can't believe he was courting myself and Rachel. How could he not realize he was courting twins until tonight? And what's up with the courting two people at once thing? I really don't understand it." Hope sat down beside her mother at the table.

"Neither do I, but I think it was a very dumb way to handle the situation. What did he tell you when he took you out to the porch?" She took her mother's hand softly as she spoke. Hope let out a short, but deep, breath.

"He broke it off with me. We're not courting anymore. I'm angry. I'm upset, mother. I have no idea what to do, and I think I yelled at Rachel for the first time." She sighed deeply this time. With no idea how to handle anything, she was all on her own. Or so she felt. She had a feeling her mother was about to rectify that.

Her mother – a wonderful woman named Faith – patted her hand softly, chuckling. There was a story coming, probably one that had to do with her courting her father. Hope didn't know a lot about her father; he had died shortly after she and Rachel had been born.

"Have I ever told you about how your father and I met, Hope?" She smiled softly. Hope shook her head. "Well, he was a local boy, came in twice a week from the town at the base of the mountain with milk. He was a sweet man, grew up into a strong man over the years." Her eyes teared up softly, as if she still missed him. She probably still did miss him. Hope knew how much her father had meant to her mother; she had never remarried. "Back then, outsiders weren't given such a favorable eye. While Richard's chances of being accepted by the community have pretty much been shot when this gets out, there are plenty of other young men in that village. Maybe you should take a day and go down there. It would mean you stayed a couple of days, but that could be very powerful."

With that, her mother excused herself, and went up to go to bed. She sat at the table as her mother's footsteps plodded away. Going down to the town at the base of the mountain is what typically passed as a rumspringa here. There wasn't a lot to explore here. Even if people made it further, they typically came back because they lived as boring a life down there as they did up here.

Hope slowly got up, turning the idea over in her head again and again. She wondered if her mother was serious. The idea of taking an early rumspringa, or even just a day trip to the town down there, was unheard of here. They lived by very strict rules. Then again, her mother had broken the rules as a young woman. Why wouldn't she continue to break rules as an adult?

She giggled softly to herself. The thought of her mother breaking a ton of laws didn't suit her. She didn't seem like the kind of woman that you would expect to be a lawbreaker. Her mother's hair sat plaited in two simple braids that ran down the sides of her body. Her hands were worn with years of providing for her and Rachel. Her eyes held the wisdom of someone decades older than she was.

Which is why Hope thought she might just be onto something. Something took over her, and she was quick to finish the dishes. The pots and pans, the plates, the cutlery, everything was finished within an hour. She then hurried up to her room. They were lucky enough that she and Rachel didn't have to share a room.

As she shut the door to her room, so that she could peel off her dress and climb in bed in her shift, she started to wonder if her mother would have to help her pack up and leave. That is, if she even decided to go. There was a good chance that, after a proper night's rest, she wouldn't feel so vile towards Richard. She hated to admit it, but there it was.

She took in a deep breath. There was no need to get all uppity about it now. The deed was almost done. As she let the breath out, she found the idea of leaving the community much more appealing.

She had already had a rumspringa. She'd gone to that town before, but she hadn't stayed long. She'd explored beyond it, living alone for most of her rumspringa. Maybe this time, she could make it work for her. Make the town part of her home. The *best* part would be coming back with a man courting her – make Richard jealous.

Her smile dropped. Is that who she was? Some woman who would make men jealous if they dumped her? That wasn't the kind of woman that she wanted to be, but it was the kind of woman she was turning into. Or, at least, the kind of woman that she seemed to be turning into.

The more that she thought about it, the more she thought she needed to get out of the community. This wasn't doing her any good. If she stayed here, she feared she would only get worse. That she would become what was once her worst nightmare: the bitter spinster lady that lived off to the side of the community.

She took her dress off, and cast it aside, not caring if it wasn't hung up or put away properly. Then, she took off her petticoats. She had two of them, and wore at least one regularly. Those she didn't cast aside quite as carelessly. Instead, she folded them up gently and placed them on top of her dresser.

In just her slip and her knee-high socks, with the garters undone, she walked over to the bed. She slid under the covers, trying to ignore the feeling of pleasure she felt from the fact that she would be leaving the community tomorrow. Even if she had to fight the bishop on it, she would be leaving again tomorrow.

It was better than being an old spinster on the side of town.

She slept well that night. No tossing. No turning. Maybe it was a good thing that Richard was out of her life.

The next morning, she woke up to the sunlight outside, streaming through her windows and the curtains. Things were boiling downstairs;

she heard bubbles popping and things being sloshed. Someone was cooking breakfast. She wondered if it was her mother; certainly smelled like her mother's cooking.

She got off her bed, and got dressed. First the petticoats and her garters. Then, she pulled a dress on over it all. This dress was blue, soft, and lighter in color than the one she had been wearing the day before. She had been fine in that one for a couple of days, but she needed a better look if she was going into town.

"Hope? Are you awake?" Her mother's voice came into the room. "Hope?"

"Yeah, I'm awake, and dressed. So, the idea you came up with yesterday...about me going into town... do you want me to act on it?" She turned to face the door as it opened. Her mother came in, and quickly smiled.

"If that's what you want to do, of course you can act on it. I'll gladly let you." She smiled a little wider. "Here. Let's get you packed up and ready to go. If you leave before Rachel wakes up, I doubt she'll ask about it."

With that, her mother helped her pack up the few clothes she had. She put the rest of the dresses in the bag. Her mother went down to the kitchen and returned with some food and water. When she gave her a questioning look, she saw that it wasn't just any food. It was her mother's recipe for one of her favorite foods that packed easily. She'd had the same thing on her first day of the rumspringa.

The bag felt heavy on her back. Maybe it was the burden of knowing that she was leaving, and possibly for good this time. Maybe it was the fact that she knew that she was breaking rules that made the bag feel heavier to her this time. She didn't know why. It was the same amount of stuff that she had packed for her rumspringa. Then, it hadn't felt nearly so heavy to her.

"Thank you, mother." She smiled softly. Her mother nodded, holding her hand.

"Be safe, honey, and make it there quickly. I know the trails get a little soggy and muddy at this time of year, but I want you to be careful and make it to town as fast as you can. You don't have to come back until you're ready to come back. I'm okay with that. I know what challenges you face, and oh, I wish I could help you more." Her mother hugged her tight. "Now go. I love you."

"I love you too, mother." Hope smiled softly at her. "Thank you, again." With that, she hurried to the front door.

She didn't remember a lot about how to get down to the town. What she remembered was that someone – years ago – had planted wooden markers all along the trail from their community to the main trail that led to town. She had to follow those now overgrown, leafy, and hard to spot markers for a good five or six miles down the mountain. She wasn't sure how she felt about that. If she felt up for that particular part of the journey yet.

It didn't matter if she was up for it. As she walked down the road, with the sun only beginning to crest the horizon, she realized she had to do it. She continued walking, her boots plopping in the mud. It must have rained the night before.

As Hope walked, she listened to the sounds of the nature around her. She heard the birds beginning to chirp, and the flip-flap of their wings as they opened and closed, getting ready for the day. She heard the crickets chirping, singing their last notes for the night. The cicadas had already become quiet, leaving an empty void in the chorus this morning.

She saw the first sign. They were every mile or so. She'd already walked a mile from the community, sharing her thoughts with no one but herself. She reveled in the quiet. It didn't happen often enough, in her opinion, the quiet.

The sun began to filter in through the leaves, illuminating her path. She played a game of stepping stones, stepping in the patches of light and shadow alternatively. First, the light patch, the one of warmth and coziness. Then the patch of shadow, the one of cold feeling and hard shivers.

As Hope walked, she began to work out what she was going to do while she was in town. If she remembered correctly, she had not met many people from the town the first time. No, it had only been a quick stopover for the night with a friend of her father's. She had only met him, and his family. He had a lovely wife and three lovely daughters. No sons. Not that she had met, anyway.

After that, she had left the town, early in the morning. So early, in fact, that she hadn't had a chance to stop at the grocery store or anything. She'd almost stayed to get some more supplies, but decided against it. She didn't have any money, anyway.

The trip went quickly this time around. Maybe that was because she already knew the way down to the town. Around the large tree – which acted as the halfway mark – and then down the rest of the trail from the community. Once she hit the main trail, it was marked out nicely and had little dips from years of being walked up and down.

This part of the trip was harder. She had to be careful; a single misplacement of her foot would send her tumbling down the mountain, possibly into the forest that surrounded her on all sides. That wouldn't be good at all. People from her community didn't come to this trail often. Those from the town at the base of the mountain didn't come this far up the mountain.

There was a good patch of orange trees that ripened around this time of year in the middle of the forest. The townspeople would come up and pick them to take back down the mountain. She'd picked the same patch the year she had gone on her rumspringa. She had enjoyed those oranges; every now and then, she'd be able to sneak away when they were ripe and pick them from the trees.

She recognized the area now. She was near those orange trees.

She broke off the main trail, and started on the rugged trail to those orange trees. Maybe having a couple of these citrus fruits would help her feel better, more at ease about the whole thing. If that was so, she didn't want to take a chance without it. If it didn't work, she hadn't lost anything but her breakfast.

There was a sudden rustling in the forest. She turned to look around her. Maybe one of those other people from the town was here.

"Hello?" She called out. Maybe she was just hearing things. Or maybe it was an animal.

"I-Is someone there?" Another voice echoed in the area nearby. "I'm stuck." She held back a giggle. "Hello?!"

"My name is Hope. What's your name?" She used the echo, or tried to use it, to find where he was stuck.

"David." Each time he spoke, she managed to find another foothold to hold onto as she looked. "That's a pretty name, by the way. I like it."

"Thank you." She felt a blush on her face. "How did you get stuck up here?" She found where he was; stuck in a ditch. "Or...down there, I guess?" He laughed a little. It must've been a funny story for him to be laughing.

"I tripped over a root." He sheepishly rubbed the back of his neck. "Do you think you can find something to lower down so I can climb out?"

She got down on her stomach and offered him her hand. He managed to grab it.

"Alright. On the count of three, I want you to jump as hard as you can. That should give me leverage to pull you out with. Sound good?" She grabbed onto his hand with her free one. He nodded slowly. "Okay. One...two...three!" He jumped hard, and she pulled on his hand as hard as she could. They both ended up back against a tree.

She was between him and the tree, her dress and petticoats flung over her knees from the force.

"Thank you, Hope." David smiled at her widely. "I've been stuck in there for two days. Do you know of somewhere I could rest while I recover?"

"Yeah, but neither option is rather close. We can go up the mountain, or down it. I think you'd rather go down, isn't that right?" She helped him stand up.

"Yeah. If possible. I know of somewhere we can stay in the town down at the base of the mountain. I think there's an Amish community up there...they probably wouldn't give us shelter; we're outsiders." He smiled at her a little more. "You heading home, then?"

"Yeah. You could say that." She smiled back just a little more. "You could say that." Then, they began down the mountain, arm in arm.

bonus story:

Ruth smiled as she stood beside the front door of the schoolhouse and watched her students file out one by one with their parents in tow. Another year and another successful Parents Day. She couldn't help but feel proud of herself, especially after spending most of the week tending to every minor catastrophe that threatened to derail the event. Some were under her control, but others, like the impending snow storm, were not.

Ruth leaned to her right and looked out the doorway and upward to the sky. The temperature had dropped considerably since that morning and gray clouds continued streaming in from the west. The snow wasn't due to arrive until the weekend, which gave her and the other residents in her small Amish community only three days to prepare. Thankfully though, it was the last day of school before the two-week Christmas break, and she could breathe a little bit easier, knowing her students would be safe at home with their parents and not traipsing back and forth to school.

"I would bet one of my sweet potato pies that will never happen."

The statement was followed by giggles, and Ruth strained an ear to listen in on the conversation between two of her students' mothers, who were standing near the end of the line. She would recognize Abigail Gandy's voice anywhere, and she was intrigued over what she was betting against one of her pies, which were talked about around their town almost as much as old man Brennan's famous peanut brittle.

"*Yah*, if it does happen, it will be a miracle," Abigail continued. "Time is certainly not on her side."

Hmm...interesting.

"I thought she might have a chance when she dated Amos Wright," the other woman, Naomi Simmons, added. "But he said she was too set in her ways to marry anyone."

Ruth inhaled sharply. Amos Wright had dated only one woman she was aware of and that woman was *her*.

"*Yah*, I suppose she will be an old maid to her dying day," Abigail replied.

The realization they were talking about her made Ruth's blood boil from anger, but worse than that, it embarrassed her. She shouldn't have been surprised, since Abigail and Naomi were two of the worst gossip mongers in town – a fact that hadn't changed since the three of them attended school together many years prior.

Their attempt at whispering was juvenile, at best, and they were so loud she was certain the other parents were overhearing the conversation. As the heat rose to her cheeks, Ruth bit her tongue to keep from lashing out.

Lord, please give me strength and please keep my temper in check.

When the two women finally caught up to her in line, Ruth held her head high and mustered as big a smile as she could manage.

"Ruth, it was so good seeing you," Naomi gushed. "I hope you have a wonderful Christmas holiday."

She returned the sentiment, and when Naomi held out a hand to shake hers. Ruth tried not to squeeze too tightly, although she would've given anything to see the look on her face if she cut off the circulation to her fingers. It would serve her right.

Ruth took a deep breath. *Come on, Lord...teach me to show these women some mercy or I'm going to do something I'll regret.*

No sooner had Ruth let go of Naomi's hand when Abigail was wrapping her arms around her shoulders and pulling her in for a hug. "Have a blessed Christmas, Ruth."

The fact that they were gossiping about her just minutes before their boisterous display of affection left a bad taste in her mouth, and Ruth pushed her away as gently as she could.

"*Denki.* I hope the two of you have a happy Christmas too," she replied.

The two women couldn't leave the schoolhouse fast enough, and as soon as they crossed the threshold, Ruth closed the door and locked it securely behind them. Leaning against it for support, she took another deep breath and fought back the sudden urge to cry.

Old maid.

Unfortunately, it wasn't the first time she'd heard someone refer to her by that phrase. Being thirty years old and unmarried in their community was very uncommon, but it wasn't as if she hadn't tried to find a suitable husband. Perhaps if there weren't such slim pickings amongst the men in her town, she would've had better luck.

Ruth took one last stroll around the room, straightening desks and gathering papers that needed storing until after the Christmas break. Despite the joy that came from celebrating the Savior's birth, she couldn't help but feel a small sense of dread too. The holiday brought along with it a multitude of different emotions, including loneliness, since she had no family to spend it with.

Ruth sat at her desk and mindlessly thumbed through the mail she'd brought from home. She knew she should be on her way, especially with the temperature dropping so quickly, but she just couldn't make herself rush toward a house where there was no one to greet her. At least at school, she felt some semblance of belonging.

A bright yellow envelope addressed from a Keith Avery in California caught her attention. Ruth furrowed a brow. The name wasn't familiar, but she received several pieces of junk mail every week, mostly from people and companies trying to sell her school supplies, so it wasn't uncommon to see a name she didn't recognize. As Ruth tore open the envelope, she was delighted to discover it wasn't junk after all – it was an actual handwritten letter.

Dear Miss Drennan,

Hello. My name is Keith Avery, and I'm an elementary school principal from Pasadena, California. I received word from our mutual friend, Nicole Turner, that you were in search of a new teaching position. We have two Amish children in our private school system, and I would love for you to visit and see if this job might be of interest to you. Enclosed you will find my business card. If you are interested, please contact me by calling the phone number provided on the card so we can discuss the details. I look forward to hearing from you.

Sincerely,

Keith Avery

How strange. Nicole never mentioned anything about a teaching job on Ruth's last visit to Lancaster, where Nicole, the only English woman she referred to as a close friend, operated a high-end clothing store.

Ruth turned the envelope over and a blue business card tumbled out onto her desk. Although she'd never considered leaving town, the invitation couldn't have come at a better time. Ruth picked up the card and twirled it around with her fingers, going over every pro and con she could think of. The thought of flying to California was both terrifying and exciting, since she'd never flown before or stepped across the Pennsylvania state line.

Ruth thought back to the conversation between Abigail and Naomi and her resolve strengthened. Why not? It wasn't as if she had a reason to stay in Lancaster anyway, other than her teaching job, and her assistant, Paige, could take over that position with no problem. There were no close friends or family members to tie her here either.

Ruth tucked the card inside her dress pocket and stood to leave. Perhaps a change of scenery was exactly what she needed, but there was only one way to know for sure. She placed a hand against her chest as the realization made her heart race out of control.

She was going to California.

* * * *

Keith craned his neck for the hundredth time as he waited for Ruth Drennan to make her appearance in the airport waiting room. The small space was filled to overflowing with people waiting for passengers, and Ruth was one of the last to walk through the doorway.

She was the only person in the room wearing a long blue dress and bonnet, so there was no mistaking her.

Keith waved his hand in the air as he struggled to get to her through the mass of people hugging each other. She looked out of place and very frightened, and her "deer in the headlights" expression tugged at his heart.

"Miss Drennan?" he called.

She smiled as he approached her, and he was instantly struck by the way her blue eyes sparkled. Her long blonde hair was tied with a ribbon at the nape of her neck, and she had the most flawless complexion he'd ever seen. Nicole once made a comment about Ruth's "understated beauty", but it wasn't understated at all. She was downright beautiful.

"Please, call me Ruth," she replied, as she held out a hand to greet him. "Are you Keith Avery?"

Her skin was soft to the touch, and he didn't want to let go, but he felt like he should show her some type of identification. He was, after all, a stranger, and the last thing he wanted to do was spook her. Keith pulled his wallet from his back pocket and opened it to reveal his driver's license. She glanced at his picture on it and nodded.

"Thank you for getting here so soon," he remarked. "Nicole has told me some wonderful things about you."

She looked genuinely surprised, and when she blushed, he felt his heart pitter-patter a little more rapidly.

"*Denki*. I'm happy to be here."

After spending most of the night studying a crash course in the Pennsylvania Dutch language, he understood *denki* to mean "thank you", and he smiled as he motioned toward the exit that would lead them to the baggage claim area.

Nudging his way through the throng of people, who were headed in the same direction, while also trying to keep from losing Ruth in the crowd, was quite the task. Christmas music blared from the overhead speakers, and with the holiday less than a week away, the airport was busting as the seams with people arriving to spend the holiday with family and friends.

"I've never seen so many people in one place," she said.

Her eyes were as big as silver dollars as she took in the sights around her, and her sense of wonder and innocence was endearing. It was rare for him to come across someone in his line of work who wasn't loud and overbearing, so her presence was certainly a welcomed change of pace.

"I wish I could tell you it's just because of the holiday, but I'm afraid it's always this way."

She smiled at his remark, and they spent the next few minutes in silence while Keith retrieved her luggage and helped guide her toward the exit that would take them to the parking lot. When they stepped outside, he took a deep breath of fresh air before showing her to his vehicle.

"It's really beautiful here...and a lot warmer than Lancaster."

Keith opened the trunk and placed her bags inside. "Our winters are pretty mild. You'll probably see a lot of palm trees decorated with Christmas lights and ornaments while you're in town."

His comment made her laugh and the soft sound of her laughter made his heart race again. When they got inside the small car, he was suddenly very much aware of how close they were, and he swallowed past the lump in his throat to keep from clamming up.

"Nicole said you were in for some rough weather this weekend. I'm glad you were able to make it out in time."

He put the car in reverse, and he couldn't help but notice the way she gripped the seat. He knew she probably wasn't used to riding in anything other than a horse and buggy, so he went slower than usual and tried not to scare her.

"*Yah*. I am too. It was just starting to snow when I boarded the plane," she replied. "I'm sorry, but I have to ask...how do you and Nicole know each other?"

Keith chuckled as he steered the car out of the parking lot and into the oncoming traffic that would take them east toward the hotel where Ruth would be staying.

"Her husband, Dan, and I went to college together. We were roommates for a couple of years before we graduated. He met Nicole while he was working as a security guard at a fashion show in Los Angeles, and he went with her back to Pennsylvania. We've kept in touch ever since, and I try to visit them at least once or twice a year."

He stole a glance in her direction, and he saw the way she nibbled on her lower lip while he drove. She stared straight ahead and he could tell she was nervous by the way the vein throbbed on the left side of her neck. He was overcome by the urge to reach out and hold her hand, but he shook his head fervently to clear his thoughts.

Stop being stupid, Keith. You just met her.

"Do you want to go straight to the hotel or would you like to visit the school first?" he asked.

That seemed to relax her somewhat. "I would love to see the school, if you don't mind."

Keith nodded and moved over to the far-right lane so he could take the next exit, while Ruth kept her eyes shut tightly the whole time. She gripped the seat so hard her knuckles turned white, but he didn't say anything. She was obviously terrified of the traffic, and he couldn't blame her. If he'd been a stranger to their state, it would've scared the daylights out of him too, so he kept quiet. She didn't open her eyes again until he'd taken the exit onto a two-lane road that was practically deserted.

"I didn't consider until after I mailed the letter that you might not have a way to contact me, but Nicole said you have a...community phone? I believe that's what she called it."

He felt embarrassed asking such a question, but the Amish way of life fascinated him, and he wanted to learn more about it if she would allow him the opportunity. When Ruth smiled at him, he gave her a tentative smile in return.

"We don't have cell phones or landline phones in our homes, but we have one community phone that everyone uses. It's located in the middle of town in a little building called a shanty that keeps it safe from the weather."

She said it so nonchalantly, as if everyone had a phone shanty, and her innocence tugged at his heart once more. She finally let go of the seat and flattened her palms against her legs, and he was happy to see some color had returned to her cheeks. As he pulled into the drive at the school, her face lit up in the biggest grin he'd seen since her arrival.

Keith brought the vehicle to a stop in front of the building, and Ruth leaned forward and stared out the front window. She was speechless at first, but it didn't take long before her excitement took over. "I've never seen such a huge building before. How many children attend school here?"

They got out of the car and Keith locked the doors behind him as they walked over to the sidewalk in front of the building. "This building houses kindergarten through sixth grade, and I believe there are roughly seven-hundred students enrolled. Seventh and eighth grade were moved to the high school building a couple of years ago. It's located about a mile from here."

Her jaw slacked but no words came out. The building was set apart from the other structures around it, including the gymnasium, playground, cafeteria, and the football field across the road from the school. Ruth made a complete circle as she tried to take it all in, while he stood by and enjoyed watching her reaction.

"Are we allowed to go inside?" she asked.

Keith dug through his front pants pockets and removed the set of keys that would unlock the building, and when he opened the door for her and turned on the overhead lights, Ruth gave him a shy smile before entering. When she walked past him, the faint scent of lavender drifted past his nose and made him weak in the knees.

"Could you please remind me what grade I would be teaching?"

It was one thing to try and get used to her stunning beauty, but quite another to get used to her friendliness and down-to-earth personality. The women he usually dealt with were rude and high-maintenance, so being with a soft-spoken woman wasn't something he was familiar with. Keith started walking down the long corridor toward the sixth-grade classrooms, and Ruth fell in step beside him.

"Our sixth-grade English teacher, Mrs. Moore, retired a couple of weeks ago, and we need someone to fill her spot. I'll show you to her classroom. It's at the end of this hallway."

He didn't get in a rush, as he enjoyed watching Ruth admire everything around her. She stopped every so often to peek inside a classroom and her whole face would light up. It was like watching a child open presents on Christmas morning.

"Do you have family back home in Lancaster?" he inquired.

Ruth stuffed her hands inside the front pockets on her dress and for the first time since she stepped off the plane, he detected a bit of sadness in her beautiful blue eyes. He immediately wanted to kick himself for asking such a personal question.

"*Neh*. My parents passed away a few years ago, and I have no brothers or sisters to speak of. The few extended family members I have live in Ohio, and I rarely see them."

Keith didn't know what to say at first. His parents, sister, brother-in-law, and two nieces lived within driving distance of his home, and he couldn't imagine being apart from them. He wanted to ask Ruth if she would be returning home in time for Christmas, but there was something inside him that told him not to. The last thing he wanted to do was make her upset, so he decided from then on to steer clear of subjects dealing with family.

Keith stopped at the last classroom on the right and opened the door to Mrs. Moore's old classroom. Ruth clapped her hands together excitedly as she walked from desk to desk and looked at everything in the room. Thankfully, Mrs. Moore left her decorations, so the classroom was brightly lit in a myriad of assorted colors from the wall decorations to the painted tiles on the floor.

"What a beautiful classroom!" she remarked. "How many children would I be teaching if I accepted the job?"

Keith sat down on top of one of the desks and went over the numbers in his head. "There are four sixth-grade homeroom classes, with at least 25 to 30 children per class, so you would be teaching at least a hundred children each day. They reciprocate between English, math, history, and science classes all day, except when they're in the cafeteria or at recess."

He could see the wheels turning in her head, and he was worried he may have bombarded her with too much information at once, but she didn't seem anxious at all. If anything, she seemed even more thrilled.

"Do you have children attending school here?"

A part of Keith secretly hoped she was asking because she was curious if he was single or married, but he tried not to get his hopes up. He hadn't spent much time with the Amish, but he did know they rarely dated outside their faith.

"No children of my own. Just two nieces – one in first grade and the other in fourth."

Ruth slid into one of the desks and made herself comfortable. "I'm surprised there are Amish children going to school here since our people don't usually settle in California."

Keith joined her, but he didn't try to squeeze his 6'2" frame into one of the small desks. Instead, he leaned against it and crossed his arms over his chest. "There's only one family that I know of. They moved here last year and the parents manage a very successful furniture business. Their twin daughters are in sixth grade."

She nodded and smiled, but she grew quiet for several minutes. Keith could tell she had a lot on her mind by the distant look on her face as she gazed around the room, but he didn't interrupt her train of thought. He knew asking her about the teaching position would be a long shot, but he heard so many good things about her from Nicole, he had to at least give it a shot.

"Did the children have trouble fitting in here?" she asked.

There was a hesitant look in her eyes, and Keith couldn't help but wonder if she was asking the question mainly to try and gauge if *she* would be accepted into the fold or not.

"The girls have done great since day one. The other children love them, and the teachers have a very good relationship with their parents too."

That seemed to lift her spirits and she smiled as she looked around the room one more time before standing. "I guess I have a lot to think about."

Keith stood too, and as they walked out of the room together, he tried not to get his hopes up. The double doors opened at the other end of the hallway, and he was caught off guard when Ruth suddenly grabbed his arm and held on tight. "Who is that?" she whispered.

He tried not to laugh, but it was hard not to. "It's just our janitor, Mr. Owens. He comes every Saturday to mop the floors."

Her cheeks turned a bright shade of red when she looked down and realized she was holding fast to his arm, but she didn't step away as quickly as he figured she would. Her body was soft and warm against his, and for a moment they simply stared at each other. When she finally let go and took a step back, the void he felt was unmistakable.

They walked the hallway in silence until they reached Mr. Owens, who stopped to introduce himself to Ruth. The fear he saw in her eyes just minutes before was replaced by a huge smile as she reached out to shake the old man's hand.

Maybe...just maybe...she would say yes to California after all.

* * * *

Ruth stood on the balcony of her hotel room and sipped a cup of coffee while the sun made its debut in the east. Another day was dawning and she still hadn't given Keith an official answer. He offered to take her on a tour of the county, and they spent most of the previous day traveling the coastline. Each destination left her more amazed than the one before it, but by the end of the day she felt something entirely different.

Guilt.

If her neighbors could see her riding in Keith's car, listening to music on the radio, drinking lemonade and buying lunch from what he referred to as a "food truck", they would be shocked. The interaction between the two of them was perfectly innocent, but she still went to bed feeling ashamed. Keith had acted like a gentleman from the very start, but she would be lying if she said her attraction to him was strictly platonic.

Ruth knew the feeling probably wasn't mutual, but it didn't stop her from daydreaming. Keith Avery was a handsome man, and it wouldn't surprise her one bit if he had a slew of women at his beck and call. They'd had a wonderful time together since she arrived, and the conversation had never flowed more freely between her and another man, but she knew the possibility of them dating was highly unlikely. On the other hand, what did she have to return to in Lancaster? If Keith wasn't in the picture, would she still want to stay in California?

Ruth sighed. The answer was a resounding yes. Everyone she'd been introduced to had welcomed her with open arms, and she could see herself teaching at the school. But did she want to risk being shunned by her community back home if she decided to live among the English?

A knock on the door stirred her from her reverie and Ruth's footsteps – and heart – were heavy as she went to answer it. There were so many decisions that needed to be made, and it was her last day in California. Her time was running out.

Ruth looked through the peephole and her heart flip-flopped inside her chest when she saw Keith standing on the other side of the door. She smoothed her hair down with the palm of her hand and straightened the apron on her dress before turning the knob.

"*Guder mariye*," she called. "I'm sorry. That means 'good morning'."

Keith laughed. "Good morning to you too. I'm sorry to bother you. I know it's early."

Ruth stood to the side and motioned for him to enter. "I'm usually up by five o'clock, so you're not bothering me at all. Would you like some coffee?"

Keith stuck his hands inside the front pockets of his slacks before walking into the room. "Sure. That would be great. Thank you."

Ruth hesitated. Something about his demeanor was...off. He seemed shy and apprehensive for some strange reason. Perhaps it was just being alone inside the hotel room with her that bothered him. Oddly enough, she wasn't troubled by it at all. She could just imagine the look on Abigail and Naomi's faces if they caught the two of them alone together, and the thought made her giggle.

While she went to the coffee maker to pour him a cup of coffee, Keith walked over to the sliding glass door and stepped out onto the balcony. He looked quite handsome in his dress slacks and blue dress shirt, and the masculine aroma of his cologne filtered through the room and made her sigh contentedly.

Ruth refilled her coffee and cautiously carried the two steaming cups to the balcony. When Keith saw her coming, he took one from her hand and moved over so she could stand beside him. Christmas was only two days away, but you couldn't tell it by the temperature. Not only that but people were walking around in shorts, t-shirts, and sandals.

"I still can't believe Christmas is almost here," she said.

Keith took a sip of his coffee and followed her gaze to the family playing around the hotel swimming pool below them. "I might say the same thing if I was in Lancaster right now. I'd probably freeze to death."

Ruth laughed out loud as she tried to imagine him trudging through the snow. They sipped their coffee in silence for a few minutes, but it was a comfortable quiet that sank in her bones and warmed her soul. She would certainly miss the sunny weather if she decided to return home. It was too bad she couldn't bottle it up and take it with her wherever she went.

"I have something for you," he said.

Ruth's heart raced as Keith removed a small box from his pants pocket.

"It's nothing big. Just a little something to remind you of California in case you decide to go back home to Pennsylvania."

Ruth set her cup on the balcony's brick railing and carefully removed the red ribbon tied to the box. When she opened it, and discovered a California-shaped refrigerator magnet inside, she didn't know whether to laugh or cry.

"Now every time you go to your refrigerator, you'll have a little reminder of your time here, and you won't forget me."

Ruth smiled as she ran her fingertips over the magnet. It was such a sweet, endearing sentiment, and it was also the first gift she'd ever received from a man – besides her father.

"*Denki*, Keith," she replied. "I love the thought behind it, but I could never forget you – even if I tried. That won't happen."

She wasn't lying. No matter what her decision might be, she would always remember her first time in California with a smile – and she certainly wouldn't forget him. From his black hair to his green eyes and muscular build, Keith Avery was impossible to forget.

"So, I'm guessing you've decided to decline the offer?"

There was no mistaking the sadness in his voice, and it gripped her heart and wouldn't let go.

"I haven't made a decision yet. This is a lot harder than I expected it would be."

The sound of children laughing drifted up to the balcony and made Ruth wonder if she would ever be blessed to hear such a beautiful sound in her own home. She and Keith were from two different worlds and there was no one waiting for her at home either. She would lose no matter what she chose to do, and the realization was a bitter pill to swallow.

"Is there anything I can do to make it easier for you?" he asked.

Ruth wished he could. "You've already done so much. You welcomed me here and treated me like family from the very beginning, but if I stay, I will never be able to return to my community, so you can see what I'm up against."

Keith placed his cup on the balcony beside hers and leaned against the sliding glass door.

"Can I ask you something? If you stay here, will that change your faith in God? Will your relationship with Him come to an end?"

Ruth looked down and shuffled her feet against the concrete. "Of course not, but...what if being here changes *me*?"

When Keith moved from his stance by the door and grabbed her hands, the sudden movement caught her off guard. She took a step back, but when she bumped against the railing she realized there was nowhere else to go. His hands were hot and the warmth from them sent a chill up her spine. She couldn't move – couldn't breathe.

"We all face the same choices every day to follow the ways of the world or remain true to who we are. This world won't change you unless you allow it to happen. No one can take your faith from you, Ruth. That's something you will always have...no matter where you live."

He spoke with such passion it was impossible not to feel it, and they stood so close she could see the rapid way his chest rose and fell with each breath. For a long while neither of them spoke, and his gaze was so steady she thought for a moment he might kiss her, which made her even more nervous. When he brought her hands to his lips and gently kissed them both, she thought for certain her heart had stopped beating.

"It's your choice, and I will accept whatever you decide to do," he whispered. "Now...I'll leave you alone so can have some peace and quiet to think."

Ruth sighed.

If only it was that simple.

* * * *

Keith wore a hole in his rug as he paced back and forth inside his living room that afternoon. He'd done everything he could think of to stay busy and take his mind off Ruth, but so far nothing was helping. He figured she would call long before now, but it was nearing six o'clock and all was quiet. Keith picked up his cell phone from the coffee table and checked to make sure he hadn't accidentally set it on silent, but the volume was as high as it could go, so he hadn't missed any calls.

He groaned as he flopped down on the sofa. He always considered himself a strong, independent man, but one tiny Amish woman from Lancaster, Pennsylvania had shown him in just three days how easily it was to bring him to his knees. He felt like a teenager again – waiting on a phone call from the perfect girl that might possibly change his life.

A loud honk outside caught his attention, and Keith scrambled to the foyer, ready to tell whoever it was to go away so he could be alone and continue pining for Ruth's phone call.

Geez. It sounded pathetic even in his head.

Keith flung open the front door, and his heart fell to his feet when he saw Ruth standing on his doorstep. He caught the fading taillights of a yellow taxi retreating down his driveway, which surprised him.

"My first taxi ride," she said. "I bet I won't forget that either. Do they all drive like maniacs?"

He chuckled as he opened the door to let her in. He could just imagine her gripping the backseat of the taxi on the long drive from the hotel to his house.

"Some of them aren't so bad," he replied. "How did you know where to find me?"

As they walked to the living room, Ruth pulled his business card from her dress pocket, and he smiled, having forgotten he'd slipped it inside the envelope along with his letter.

"I was going to call you from the hotel, but the more I thought about it, the more I realized this should be done face-to-face."

The tone of her voice made his spirits wilt. She sounded so serious, and that could only mean one thing – she'd decided to decline the teaching job. He gestured to the sofa, and his feet felt like lead as he tried to make the short walk so he could sit down.

Perhaps she was right. At least, with her coming to his house, they would have the opportunity to say goodbye in person instead of over the phone, which would've felt cold and impersonal.

She sat down beside him and he didn't miss the way she took a couple of deep breaths before speaking.

He swallowed. This was going to be bad.

"I've thought a lot about what you said this morning and you're right. Where I live doesn't determine my faith…I do. I can worship God wherever and whenever I want to…and I want to do that here. Everyone is so nice, and the teaching position is a dream come true. I truly feel like this is meant to be my new home."

Keith had never felt so relieved. He was overcome with the sudden urge to kiss her, but he also didn't want to startle her by rushing, so he kept his place. When Ruth leaned into him and kissed him first, he was completely caught off guard…but in a good way. It was a brief kiss, but he felt the ripple of it from the top of his head to the tips of his toes.

"I'm sorry," she whispered. "I hope I'm not being too forward."

He smiled before returning her kiss. Her lips were so soft, and when he deepened the kiss, he felt her body tremble. When they parted, he noticed her breathing was labored – much like his own.

"I've wanted to do that since the first time I saw you at the airport," he replied. "I apologize if that's being too forward too."

They both laughed.

"Does your school board have rules against the principal dating a teacher?"

Keith kissed her forehead, nose, and then both cheeks before brushing his lips against her mouth. "No," he answered. "But even if they did, I'm sure we could find some way around it...together."

Ruth rested her head against his shoulder and he heard her sigh as he held her close against his body. He couldn't help but smile as he thought about the many things they would be able to experience as a couple now that she had decided to stay.

"Together," she replied, softly. "I like the sound of that."

UNDER THE AMISH TREES

TERRI DOWNES

It had been a while since the last barn raising, and Matthew had almost forgotten how much he enjoyed them. The social element was fun, but it was working together, building something, that felt so good, that uplifted his soul and left it singing.

It had been hot today, and he felt sticky with sweat and tired all the way through, in a way that hinted at some stiffness tomorrow. Not much, as Matthew had plenty of heavy lifting to do every day at the farm, and he would be in a poor state if a barn raising set him back too much.

Still, he would sleep very well tonight... and he needed something cold.

The table that had been used to serve lunch had been cleared earlier, but there were jugs of water and iced tea set up at one end, being poured out by the expansively beaming Mrs. Annie Simon, who seemed thrilled at her family's new barn. As Matthew approached the table, however, he heard a baby start crying somewhere in the house. Annie stepped away from the table with a worried expression and beckoned to another of the women to take over from her.

Matthew's insides gave a jump as he saw who now stood at the table; his mouth, already dry, felt as though it were full of sand.

"Water – " his voice came out as a croak and he coughed hastily. "Um, water, please – " no better.

Lovina smiled politely at him.

"You sound like you've been wandering in the desert," she commented, placing an invitingly condensed glass of water before him.

Matthew drank half of it before he answered.

"Not quite that dire," he said.

He did not tell her that he had, in fact, once spent time in a desert, and had felt the dry, searing heat envelop him as though he had just opened the world's largest oven door, and that he had slept under the stars, which had been far more beautiful than he had been able to appreciate at the time.

Such things were not to be spoken of between them.

"Tiring work," Lovina added, nodding towards the almost-finished barn.

Matthew nodded. And then, unbidden, her words recalled a memory long buried. He grinned.

"Yes," he said recklessly, "but it's the *most best* kind of tired."

Lovina paused for a moment – then laughed, her face lighting with recognition. But then she looked over Matthew's shoulder, and her face fell. She frowned. Turning, Matthew followed her gaze, and saw his cousin.

Thomas was leaning back against a gatepost across the yard. His posture was languid and rakish, his smile almost a smirk, as he talked to the girl standing beside him. The girl who Matthew recognized now as Lovina's sister Tessa.

He watched the pair for a moment, wondering... he could not see anything obviously untoward. He turned back to Lovina, but she had already started busying herself with putting the dirty glasses in a tub to be washed, and he knew that the small moment they had shared, an echo of so many others, was over.

***

Whoompf.

Bright, copper-colored shapes flew up above Matthew's head as he landed backwards in the pile of leaves, his short legs kicking up over his head in delight.

He turned and saw that Lovina had vanished, but a rustling in another pile gave away her position. A small giggle floated up.

"Lovina?" he called, pretending he did not know where she was.

Another giggle. Matthew decided that he could not be too hard on her. She was only five; he, on the other hand, was six, old enough to know that you are not supposed to giggle when you hide from people.

He walked forward quietly, placing each foot down heel-first to muffle his steps. As he reached the giggling pile, he reached down, scooped up a handful of leaves, and then jumped in front of the pile, showering them over Lovina.

"Got you!" he yelled.

She pouted, and tried to fight off the leaves as they landed on her. Matthew thought she should leave them. The orange looked nice with her pink cheeks, yellow hair and blue dress. She looked like a rainbow. He offered her a hand to help her out of the pile.

"How do you find me so fast?" she demanded.

"You have to stop laughing," explained Matthew as they walked on, Lovina occasionally darting forward to catch a leaf before it reached the ground.

It was fall, and the small beech wood that stretched along the land between their parents' farms had slowly been turning yellow and orange, brighter and brighter – until the leaves, grown heavy with color, began to fall to the ground below. Matthew and Lovina had both begged to be allowed to go play today, as the forest was exactly at that perfect moment when there was brightness both above and below, as though the forest were a golden hall in Heaven, and the leaves were still piled in big, crunchy drifts, before the rain came and washed them into mush.

Matthew had had a harder time getting permission than Lovina. She said his parents were "strict" - he was not sure what that meant, but he knew that he was not allowed to do as many things as the other children his age. Even when he had finished all his chores, he was not always allowed out, but had to sit quietly at home. Today, though, he had caught his mother in a good mood, and she had agreed.

"Are you tired?" he asked Lovina, aware that they had been playing for a while now.

"A bit," she said, pausing to step again on an especially crunchy leaf. "But it's the *most best* kind of tired."

He stopped himself from correcting her grammar, reminding himself again of her youth and ignorance.

"It is," he agreed. And Lovina, he thought, might be the most best person he knew.

***

Dusk was beginning to fall, the sky deepening into a creamy purple, by the time Matthew and Thomas reached the lane that led to home. Matthew drew in a deep breath, feeling as though he could bask in the gentle coolness and falling quiet until they reached the farmhouse.

But Thomas was antsy, as usual, and kept humming and kicking at the path as they walked, raising clouds of dust. Matthew sighed inwardly. His cousin had been staying with him for several months now, and he had yet to acquire the sense of responsibility his father had hoped the change would bring to him. Uncle Jesse had grown up a farmer, and worried that his seventeen year old son's frustration and restlessness in the family's new furniture trade was not something that he could curb by keeping him in the workshop all day. He had sent Thomas to Matthew, to the farm he had inherited after his parents had moved into his married brother's *Dawdi* house. Uncle Jesse had believed that outdoor work would be the solution, although Matthew had not been so hopeful...

As the lane took them near to Lovina's family home, Matthew cleared his throat.

"I saw you talking to Tessa earlier," he said, nodding at the house ahead as though in reference.

"Nice girl," said Thomas, grinning.

"Yes, she is," said Matthew guardedly. "As his her sister."

"Lovina's a little old for me," teased Thomas, who had seen his cousin gazing at the eldest Lapp sister at social gatherings.

"You know I don't mean Lovina," said Matthew. "You were hanging around Verity the last two weeks, and it looked like you were interested in her."

"Did it now?" said Thomas.

"And she was obviously interested in you," said Matthew, risking the dangers of boosting Thomas' vanity in order to get to the point. "So what's she going to think if you transfer your affections to her sister?"

"Who says they've transferred?" laughed Thomas, taking a few longer strides which forced Matthew to hurry. He liked reminding Matthew of the four inch difference in their heights – a difference which Matthew, at twenty-two, was unlikely to recover.

"So you're not interested in Tessa?" pushed Matthew.

"Who says I have to pick one?" asked Thomas.

Matthew blinked. Then he felt his face grow warm. "Because otherwise you're just flirting with them."

"Oh, come on," said Thomas, still striding onward through the dusk. They had nearly drawn level with the Lapp home. "They know we're just having fun."

"Just... having fun?" Matthew repeated incredulously.

"Yes, fun, remember that, Matthew?"

Thomas laughed, and then waved – the Lapps had already reached their home, and the girls were on the porch. Tessa and Verity waved back. Matthew thought that he could see Lovina looking at him, though it was hard to tell given the distance and the darkness. He raised a hand, and she returned the gesture, but there was no hint of that earlier smile in her shadowed face.

***

"Maybe we should get married."

Lovina glanced up from the jacket in her lap. "Just cause I'm doing your mending doesn't mean I'm going to marry you, Matthew."

Matthew pulled a face at her, and she rolled her eyes.

It was only fair that she should fix it the jacket, Lovina decided. It was her fault, she had asked him to climb one of the beech trees and fetch a handful of the young, spring leaves, because her brother Zach had told her you could eat them.

Matthew had panicked when he had noticed the tear. Apparently, his mother had told him that the next time he ripped something, he would not be allowed go out and play for a whole month. Lovina did not know why Matthew's mother was so worried, as Matthew was already much more careful than the other boys – definitely more careful than her little brothers Zach, Jonathan and Henry. But Lovina did not want Matthew to get stuck indoors for a month, so she had volunteered to mend his jacket with the little sewing set she had been given three months earlier, just after her eighth birthday.

"Not cause of that," said Matthew, throwing a flower at her. He had been gathering them at the edge of the wood, near where Lovina was sitting. She secretly hoped he meant to give them to her, but did not want to ask.

"Why then?" she asked, holding the jacket to the light to see the stitching.

"Cause all the others are getting all worked up about it," he said. "As soon as they grow up, it's all they think about. You heard about Sadie and Isaac."

"It's not good to gossip."

"It's not gossip, everyone knows. She threw a rock at him."

"It was a pebble."

"Still." Matthew surveyed the bunch of flowers critically. "It's something they all worry about. If we decide now, we could forget about it til it comes up again."

"Maybe..." Lovina shook out the jacket. "There you go."

"Thank you," said Matthew again, and handed her the flowers he'd picked.

"I didn't say yes," joked Lovina, though she took the flowers anyway.

****

For Lovina, trying to catch all of her siblings in one place at one time was like trying to pick up water. They had their meals together, but the boys spent that time planning what they would be doing next on the farm, and Tessa and Verity talked... well, gossiped. Sometimes the boys ate before or after their sisters, fitting meals in around their work. Lovina knew that she should impress on them how important it was to spend time with their family, but she did not know how to go about it without seeming as though she was trying to make them feel guilty.

And now, when she had told all of them individually that she needed to speak to everyone in a group, they still could barely stop long enough to listen. Verity was already gone, having walked over to a friend's house as soon as she had done her chores, and Tessa was talking about her own plans for the day. And the boys looked like they were sleepwalking. They had been working too hard, again, and Lovina did not know how to get them to slow down.

"Wait, just wait," she called out, halting the boys on their way out of the door.

"We have to – " started Zach, as Jonathan rubbed his eyes blearily and Henry yawned.

"I know, just wait a moment – Tessa, hold on just a – "

"Sadie's expecting me, we're supposed to quilt – "

"I *know*," said Lovina, a little too loudly. Her siblings all looked at her then. None of them really looked the same as each other, with slightly varied hair colors, skin tones, and statures, but they all had their mother's bright hazel eyes. Their one link.

"You know it's the anniversary soon," she said, while she still had their attention. Their expressions immediately clouded over. "I was thinking we could do something, you know, like we used to. What do you think?"

There was a brief silence. "Sure," said Henry, glancing down. The others nodded.

"All right," said Lovina, heartened, "what should we do?"

They had used to picnic by the river, to remember the anniversary of their parents' deaths, but for the last two years everyone had decided that they were too busy to give up a whole afternoon.

"Whatever you want," said Zach, shrugging. The others were already turning to leave.

"But I – "

"We have to go."

"So do I," said Tessa, and she was out of the door before Lovina could get a word out.

Walking to the window, Lovina saw the tall, rangy figure of Thomas Zehr standing at her gate, waiting for her sister. As Tessa reached him, he bent down toward her, as though he were whispering something in her ear. Tessa laughed.

Lovina closed her eyes.

Lord, I don't know what to do. I was not old enough to become a mother to all of them, but they still needed one. I don't know how to reign in my sisters. I don't know how to stop my brothers working themselves to death, trying to live up to our father's name. I don't know how I could ever marry, and leave them, but I don't know how I can keep doing this without a partner to help me.

I don't know anything.

***

"Well, look at you!"

Matthew grinned at Lovina and stepped close to her, straightening up and judging the difference between his and Lovina's height with his hand.

"You're as tall as me!"

Lovina smiled at him. She had not seen him all Summer, as he had gone to stay with his aunt's family. He had a lot of family, but none of them ever came here, though she was not sure why. He was leaner and browner than he had been in the spring, and his nut-colored hair had been lightened in the sun, but he did not appear to have grown much. Still, he looked older. Lovina felt almost shy as she met his eyes.

"Maybe I'll overtake you," she said, falling into step with him as they began their old walk through the thick green shade under the beeches. "And you'll stay the same."

"Girls get taller quicker, everyone knows that," protested Matthew. "I'll have time to catch up, I'm not even twelve yet."

"Better hurry," laughed Lovina, standing on her toes to gain a couple more inches.

"Oh, I'm in no hurry to grow up." Matthew walked ahead a little.

Lovina felt there was an undercurrent to his words, but she could not place it.

"No?"

"No," repeated Matthew, his face set. Then he saw her looking at him and smiled. "Doesn't seem like a lot of fun, does it?"

"I don't know..." Lovina thought of her home, of how loving and warm it was, with her mother running everything with her capable hands and heart. "I'm looking forward to it."

"Not too soon though," said Matthew. He looked up at the canopy above them, grown thick and dense over so very many years.

***

Lovina could not believe what she was hearing. She looked at her sisters, both watching her with their eyebrows slightly raised, expressions that said clearly they were expecting her to make a scene. To pretend to be *Mamme*, whom she could never be. Lovina swallowed.

"Isn't this a little sudden?" she asked, trying to keep her voice quiet. Trying to remain reasonable.

Verity rolled her eyes, and Lovina felt a spark of temper which she quickly tamped down.

"We've been thinking about it for a while. We just decided. Why wait?"

"But why go away at all?" asked Lovina.

She had never even thought of going away for rumspringa when she was their age. Moving away from home, living somewhere else... not like others. She pushed the memory down.

But then, she had had her parents as her center. She had always known that she wanted to be in her home, and then to start her own home, building something that would last. She had had her mother to look up to. Verity and Tessa only had their failure of a big sister.

"How will you pay for everything?" she asked, trying to stick to simple points.

"We'll get jobs," said Tessa, as this were the most obvious thing in the world.

"Where?" asked Lovina. "And how?"

"Thomas said he knows – " started Tessa, before Verity elbowed her in the side.

But Lovina already felt something choking her.

"Thomas?" she said. "Thomas *Zehr*?" Neither of her sisters would meet her eyes across the kitchen table. "He's going on this – this trip as well, is he?" Lovina heard her voice becoming shrill.

"He was going on his own trip," corrected Verity in a sulky tone, "and said he could help us. He was being nice."

"Oh, very nice," said Lovina, pushing herself away from the table and heading out of the back door. She half-expected one of her sisters to call her back, but neither of them did.

She wandered across the pasture, half-blinded by the setting sun, until she reached the edge of the beech wood. Its deep, dark interior, shot through with golden flecks as the sun made its way between the branches, looked indescribably inviting.

But Lovina could not bring herself to enter it. If she and Matthew were still close – well, she would have gone to him now, that was certain.

She sank down into the grass, burying her fingers in the tufts of green.

Lord. If they have to leave – if I have to let them go – I understand. But why must it break my heart?

If I am meant to be alone –

The thoughts stopped Lovina in her tracks for a moment and she had to take a deep breath before she continued her prayer.

– Then let me rejoice in it, Lord. Let me be as one of the apostles who found their family in the church, who did not need children, or siblings, or marriage. Please, Lord, if I am not to have these things, let me not want them any more.

Lovina sat quietly, waiting. Waiting to stop wanting. Waiting for her heart to let go of the dreams she kept coming back to. But nothing happened.

***

"How is he?"

Lovina shook her head. "They've given him orders to rest, but that's still no guarantee that it won't happen again, or that it won't get worse."

Matthew bit his lip. Lovina's father had been complaining of shortness of breath and dizzy spells for a while now, and a week ago he had passed out in the fields. It seemed strange to see Lovina looking like this, so pale and exhausted, with the appearance of someone far older than her thirteen years.

"How are your brothers and sisters?" he asked. "I guess Tessa and Verity must be taking this hard."

Lovina's sisters had always been a little too sensitive. High-strung, Lovina's mother called it. He had grown to know them well over the years, through his friendship with Lovina, and he felt strangely guilty at the fact that he could do nothing to protect them from what they were going through. Not that he did not want to protect Lovina as well, but she had been oddly withdrawn over the past week. She had been busy, of course, helping her mother run things. But Matthew had not been able to speak to her before the walk they were taking today.

And now that they were in their special place, under the beech trees – even though the branches were barren, forming cracks against the hard winter sky, the place was still a comfort – he did not feel as though he could burden her with his own problems.

As though she could tell what he was thinking, Lovina turned to him.

"What about you?" she asked. "How have you been since I saw you last, how's your family?"

Matthew opened his mouth to tell her.

Then closed it.

"Fine," he said. "Same as normal."

Well, that was the truth.

"Good," said Lovina, "that's... that's good..." her voice caught, and her face crumpled.

Matthew stood awkwardly as Lovina turned away to cry. He knew that she would be embarrassed about him seeing her like this, but he could hardly pretend that it was not happening.

"I'm fine," mumbled Lovina, burying her face in her handkerchief.

"I can tell," said Matthew, which at least made her laugh.

"I'm sorry," she said, wiping at her eyes. "I just – there's just so much, suddenly. My brothers and sisters, and my parents, they're all relying on me, and I don't know if I can handle everything."

"You can," said Matthew.

Lovina gave him a half, somewhat watered-down smile.

"And if you ever can't," he continued, "if it's ever too much, if something happens that your parents can't help you with, you just come and find me. I'll be there."

Lovina looked at him for a long moment. "Promise?" she said.

***

Matthew had decided, before beginning this conversation, that he was going to keep his temper. Amazingly, he had managed to do so. What he had not counted on, however, was Thomas being unable to keep his.

"Why can't you leave me alone?" the younger man demanded, eyes narrow and hard. "What's it got to do with you?"

"It's inappropriate," said Matthew, his tone even. "You've been flirting with both of them, openly, and – "

"And all the old folks will talk, I know, how terrible. You're worried people are going to think you were a bad influence on me?"

Matthew counted to ten inside his head before speaking. He looked at the clock on the wall of the living room so that he would not be tempted to rush.

"Won't you think of the girls, then?" he asked. "Tessa and Verity might end up with damaged reputations if you keep on as you are."

"It's not my fault if people gossip," said Thomas, his cheeks staining red. "We haven't done anything wrong, Matthew. I've never touched either of them."

"But how have you been looking at them, Thomas?" Matthew asked quietly. "Where do your thoughts about them lead you?"

Thomas broke eye contact, scowling at his feet.

"You really think I'm worried about other people's opinions?" said Matthew. "God's opinion is the only one that matters." Thomas remained silent, so Matthew tried another push. "You know that I'm the last person who could judge you – "

But at this, Thomas' head shot up. "Yes," he said, "You are the last person who could judge me. In fact, I thought you all of all people would understand, but you're just as self-righteous as the rest of them."

He pushed himself out of his chair and headed for the door.

Matthew stood and followed him to the porch, more to see where he was going than to try and start the conversation over. There would be chance for that later, when Thomas had calmed down. But as he watched Thomas heading with angry steps out into the fields, his attention was suddenly drawn by a figure standing nearer to him. At the gate – just outside the gate, looking at the house as though wondering whether to approach.

"Lovina?"

Matthew walked across the yard to her as she made her way to him, so that they met at the center. It was early evening, and the air was cool and fresh after a shower of rain a few hours before. The cloud cover had broken into large, fluffy mounds, with starkly sunlit outlines. Lovina stood in the pearly light, her face serious.

"Did Thomas tell you?" she asked. "Is that what you were arguing about?"

"You heard that?"

"I heard him yelling."

"Oh – wait." Matthew paused, frowning. "Did he tell me about what?"

Lovina broke the news to him about the plan which her sisters had let slip. As he listened, Matthew felt a surge of protection for Tessa and Verity. He had never been able to shake the feeling that they should by rights have been a part of his family, even though the hopes of that becoming a reality had long been lost.

"Thank you for telling me this," he said as she finished. "I suppose... I suppose I can send Thomas back to his parents."

"They could still meet up, if they all leave," said Lovina, shaking her head. She reached up and pinched the bridge of her nose, an action that seemed to belong to someone far older than she was.

"You can't convince the girls to stay?" asked Matthew.

He regretted the question as Lovina met his eyes with a burning gaze.

"*No*," she said. "I can't. I can't make them do anything. *I'm not my mother*."

"No one's expecting you to be your mother," Matthew said gently.

"Aren't they?" Lovina snapped. "No, no, I guess they're not, because even my mother couldn't handle everything herself, she had my father. I don't understand – "

She pinched the bridge of her nose once more, and Matthew barely heard the words that came next:

"I don't understand why I have to do this alone."

"You're not alone," he said, "I'm – " and then he stopped, realizing how similar this was to another conversation they had once had.

From the way she was watching him, Lovina had clearly made the connection as well.

" – I'm here," he finished. Because he had to.

Lovina looked at him a moment longer, then dipped her head in a nod, her mouth pressed together.

"Lovina," said Matthew, "it's not the same as it was. I'm not the same."

"Neither am I," she said.

***

"You're really going."

They had come to say goodbye, under the beech trees. Matthew had bid the Lapps a polite family farewell, but Lovina had known, somehow, that he would be waiting for her here.

Lovina was aware that she had not spoken to Matthew, not properly, in a long time. Wrapped up in her family, she had hardly had the chance, or that is what she told herself. She knew that things at his home had not been good for a long time – if ever they had been good – but she had not expected this.

He was leaving. Going away, for Rumspringa. He was getting a job somewhere, with the intention of traveling around as much of the country as he could see.

"You'll be all right," he said.

Lovina's father had not had a bad spell for a year, though he had never regained his full strength. He was training the boys to run the farm, and they had thrown themselves into it as though they could bring him back to life as they brought life from the soil.

"What about you?" she asked.

"Don't worry about me." His voice was flat and removed, as though he were saying the words by rote. As though there was no reason to think that she actually would worry about him.

When was the last time anybody worried about you, she wondered, as she watched her childhood friend turn and walk away into something he hoped would become freedom.

***

It had been hard enough to get the three of them to agree to this; Matthew had hoped that they would at least take it seriously. But Thomas was leaning his elbows on the table with an indolent air, and Tessa and Verity kept exchanging glances and smirking.

Well, there was nothing for it.

"Lovina told me what you're planning," he started.

"Why do I feel like I'm back at school...?" murmured Thomas, and the girls spluttered with laughter.

Matthew gritted his teeth for a moment. He wondered if he should have remained standing, rather than sitting opposite them.

"You know that I did something similar myself," he said.

"We know," said Tessa. "You had all of your fun, and then decided to come back and be good."

"And now you think that we should make the same decision as you, with none of the fun," said Thomas.

Matthew took a long, deep breath. He leaned back a little, and looked up at the ceiling.

"Maybe I should just let you go," he said quietly – so quietly, that he sensed the others were having to pay real attention to listen in. "But if my experiences could help someone else, then maybe they'd be worth something. Maybe some good could come out of it all."

He looked back at the three before him.

"Rumspringa can be an opportunity," he said. "For some, it is a chance to find out what it really means to make a commitment. Others find that they might be called to live a different life. Some just need to get perspective. And if I felt that your plan involved any one of these, I wouldn't say a word."

He felt his gaze harden, and a sternness crept into his voice.

"But this, what you want," he said, "is pleasure. Worldly pleasure. You don't want to try a different perspective, or build something new. You want to break all the rules you have had to live with, and forget the consequences."

Thomas opened his mouth to speak, but Matthew held up his hand.

"But what you don't know – and it is a privilege not to know this, believe me – is that there are consequences. Real dangers, and in the lifestyle you're headed toward, you're going to find them as soon as you get there."

There was a moment's silence. Verity traced a pattern on the tabletop with her finger.

"So there's a danger," she said. "But won't it be worth it? For freedom?"

You don't want freedom, thought Matthew. *You want to escape a home that is not the one you grew up so loved and coddled in, and a life that you don't want to face.*

But that was not what she needed to hear right now.

"They didn't call it freedom," he said. "The people I met. They called it something else."

He had hoped never to remember this.

"They called it oblivion." He closed his eyes. "*Total oblivion.*"

He knew, from the hush on the other side of the table, that he finally had their complete attention.

So he told them. He told of the oblivion he had found, and the people he had found it with. People who had emptiness behind their eyes, and teeth instead of smiles, whose minds had not been their own in years. Rooms that existed only in darkness, people whose lives centered only on the things that happened in those rooms. Relationships that had seemed like they meant something, only to twist themselves into nothingness. The degradation, the hopelessness of it all, the way you became bound to your body as though you were its slave, allowed only to bring it what it demanded, feeding appetites which only seemed to grow.

He told them, and they listened.

***

"Matthew?"

Matthew could not understand what he was looking at. Was it the ocean? It kept moving, he could hear it, and it was a greeny-gray color. But it was so far away. It made him feel happy. Like everything was going to be all right. And that voice, too, that made him happy.

"Matthew, I've called the boys, they're going to take you to your aunt's, I don't think you should go home like this."

Matthew felt his thoughts slowly coming back to his head. He opened his eyes all the way. Oh, right, that wasn't the sea. It was the canopy of the beech wood, and he was lying beneath it on his back.

And there was Lovina, looking at him.

Wait – Lovina?

She looked the same. Different. Older.

Matthew tried to push himself up, but Lovina was already kneeling beside him, telling him to stay still.

"You look like you'll snap in half if you try to move," she said, her voice soft.

Matthew frowned, wondering what she meant. He tried to think of what he looked like... when was the last time he had seen his reflection? He had a dim memory of a mirror in a grimy gas station bathroom, seen sometime in the last couple of days. His skin had been pale, faintly jaundiced, stretched paper thin over jutting bones. The florescent light had cast shadows in his eyes and in the hollows of this cheeks.

"How did you even get here?" he heard Lovina murmur.

"Walked," he told her. Obviously. And he smiled, because even though she had tears in her eyes, it was Lovina, and they were in the beech wood, exactly where they should be.

"My parents..." he started to say, trying to sit again.

With a gentle touch to his shoulder, Lovina pushed him down. He noticed one of his sleeves sliding up, and hastily pulled the cuff back to his wrist.

"You can go to them once you're well," said Lovina. "I think it will be all right. They've been doing better, these past couple of years. I think you leaving shook them. They've been getting help from the preachers. Counseling."

"Right. Good for them," said Matthew, smiling wryly. Yes, good for them, how nice for them. "And your parents?" he asked.

There was a pause, during which all he could hear was the swishing and hissing of leaves in the wind.

"They're dead, Matthew," said Lovina.

The words took a few moments to penetrate.

"What."

"Two years ago, a few months after you left."

Matthew shook his head. "But – no – "

"*Mamme* got sick," said Lovina. "It was sudden. When he knew she wasn't going to make it, *Daed* just gave up. They went the same night."

"No – "

This was wrong. This was not supposed to happen. He had said, he had promised –

"I said I would be here," he whispered. "I said I would be here for you."

"Yes," said Lovina. "You did say that."

And Lovina was standing, moving away from him, creating a distance between them that he would never have a right to recover.

***

He works all things together for the good.

Lovina was not sure why this verse had been buzzing around her head all morning. She had been praying as she completed her chores, and it had popped into her mind. And stayed there. Almost as though it were being said to her, over and over...

All things together for the good of those who love him.

And then, as she heard the door to the kitchen open and close, *his plans are better than yours.*

She turned, and saw Tessa and Verity. Their eyes were reddened and swollen.

Lovina nearly dropped the bowl she was holding. She could not remember the last time either of them had cried.

"What happened? What's wrong?"

"Nothing," said Verity, shaking her head. "Nothing's wrong."

***

"Thought I'd find you here."

Lovina stopped walking and turned, waiting for Matthew to catch her up. It was midday, and by rights she should have been attending to her work, but she had felt the cool green of the beech wood calling to her, for the first time in years. She had left Verity and Tessa in charge, and escaped to the shade of the canopy. The two of them had been in a whirl of baking, preparing for the picnic they were determined to have the next day, just as they used to, to remember their parents.

"Have you spoken to the girls?" asked Matthew, falling into easy step next to her. They always walked at the same pace, Lovina remembered, being the exact same height.

"They didn't want to talk too much yesterday," said Lovina, "but they told me what you'd... discussed."

"Ah."

"Thank you. For telling them. That must have been difficult."

Matthew shrugged. "It was necessary," he said, but his tone betrayed how hard he had found it. "Are they staying, then?" he asked.

"Verity is," said Lovina. "Tessa still wants to go away for a while, but she's talking about getting a real job, and we've discussed things like a self-imposed curfew, keeping in touch... she's trying to be responsible."

Matthew nodded. "Thomas is saying something similar," he said. "Though, to be honest, I get the feeling that he's not going to see it through."

"No?"

"No, I think he was just getting carried away with the idea of *no rules*. I told him to pray about it – maybe he'll still go, but I think it's going to be all right either way."

"I think you scared them straight," said Lovina, trying to be a little flippant, but Matthew's face creased.

"I'm sorry if any of it was too upsetting," he said. "I don't know how much they told you – "

"I'd guessed most of it," said Lovina. "You said some things, that day I found you here."

"I did?" Matthew ran a hand over his head and rubbed the back of his neck. "I'm sorry."

"It's all right."

"No, really, I'm sorry, for everything, Lovina." He stopped walking, his face earnest.

Lovina stopped too and shook her head, indicating that he did not need to continue, but he pressed on.

"I wasn't here," he said, "when you needed me. I let you down. I'm sorry."

He was standing close, so close, his expression open, and Lovina felt the bond between them as roots beneath the surface of the earth. Hidden, buried, never gone.

"I let you down first," she said. Because it was the truth. "You needed me, and I left you alone."

Matthew looked as though he wanted to argue, but Lovina met his gaze straight on and he hesitated. She knew that he knew she was right.

"Well, then," he said slowly. "Perhaps we should agree that we won't leave each other again."

Lovina felt a smile being pulled to the surface, as though her happiness were seeking fresh air and sunshine.

"Never again," she agreed.

And they walked on, through the warm green light that filtered down through the beech leaves.

THE AMISH ENGAGEMENT

LORI WALL

Katie sighed as she watched her younger sister, Mary, rapped her fingers on the nightstand. In her other hand, she held her worn bible.

"Mary, please don't tap your nails on the nightstand."

"Sorry, Katie." The young girl sighed, and held the bible in both hands now. She lowered it to look at her sister. "I'm bored."

"I know it's tough to be bedridden. As soon as your leg heals, you'll be able to walk again." The community doctor had told her that as soon as her leg had healed, and she could walk on her own, Mary would be able to take off and go on her *rumspringa*. She had been looking forward to it for a year; she wanted more education.

The entire community was sure that Mary would be the one who got lost before baptism. Katie had returned from hers the week before Mary's leg was broken in a freak horse-riding accident. She had found many of the boys creepy and had almost been killed once because she was in what the locals deemed a 'bad part' of town.

At any rate, she had cut hers short by two weeks and returned home. She was to be baptized the next day, but with Mary's leg, she had postponed her baptism.

"Willis comes home today." Mary spoke up again. "You know, Mark's Willis." Katie looked up. "I hear he missed you."

"Shush, Mary. You're supposed to be reading."

"You know I can't read in bed." Her sister sighed deeply. "If you're so worried, read to me." Katie picked up her own bible as her sister continued to complain. "Hey. I'm in Leviticus."

"Alright." She managed a smile. However, as she read her sister Leviticus 2 aloud, she wasn't sure how she felt. Willis M. Wittmer had always been a bit of a rowdy boy. No one had expected him to return after his *rumspringa*, but she had always felt there was something different about him. His brown hair grew too fast for his mother to keep up with it, and so he would sometimes get away with wearing his hair longer than he should have.

Either way, everyone had been incredibly excited that he was coming home. He would be getting baptized within the week, and if Mary felt she could get on without her for about an hour, she would go. She hadn't realized she had stopped reading aloud.

"Katie?" Mary's voice interrupted her thoughts. "Katie?"

"Huh?" She looked up from the pages of the bible. "What?" Her sister laughed a little, and she looked down at the bible again. It fell off her lap, and onto the floor.

"You're daydreaming, again, aren't you?" She smiled widely. "You're thinking about *Willis*. Aren't you?"

"Am I that easy to read?" She shifted uncomfortably in her chair.

"Honey, if only I could find love that easily."

"I'm not in love." She felt her cheeks becoming even hotter than they usually were. The words came out in a mutter, and she could feel her sister's eyes on her. She didn't dare to look up again.

"Katie! You have a visitor." Their mother's voice floated up the house.

"I'll be back as soon as possible, Mary." She picked the bible up off the floor before setting it on the table. Then, she walked down to the living room as quickly as possible.

"Hello, Katie." A masculine voice echoed in her ears. Her eyes fell on a buff 18 year old with familiar blue eyes.

"Willis..." She smiled a little. "How have you been?"

"Anxious to come home." He returned her smile. "And you?"

"I've had my fair share of homesickness too." She stayed on the far side of the room. "I hear you're to be baptized soon. Congratulations."

"Thank you. Have I heard correctly that you're getting baptized soon as well?" He took a couple steps closer, but still had a lot of room to cover.

"Yes." She smiled a little wider.

"Congratulations, Katie." His smile widened as well. "I should probably get going. Is Mary still bedridden?"

"Unfortunately. How did you hear?"

"My mother told me shortly after I arrived home. She told me not to bother you much today." She couldn't help but laugh a little bit.

"Thanks. I'll see you around?" He laughed a little now, nodded, and began to walk out the door. She didn't try to stop him. However, she did notice that he had changed.

Instead of being excited about being out in the world, he had said that he was anxious to come home. Anxious to come home meant that he missed something about their lifestyle. He missed something, or someone, bad enough to forgo everything he had thought he wanted after his *rumspringa*. Not only that, but he had bulked up while he was away. Even with daily work on the farm, the men in her community weren't too muscular or strong. More often, they had the bare minimum so that they could do their job without being sore all day, every day.

He'd also grown taller. Willis had been slightly taller than her when she left; now he was about a foot taller. His smile had become a little more radiant, and he was no longer itching to get away from their lifestyle.

Katie returned upstairs slowly, thinking over his words and turning them around and around in her head. In her long blue dress, she certainly had no attractive features to show off except for the light dusting of freckles across her cheek and nose, and her light brown eyes. Her parents often said that if her commitment to their lifestyle didn't attract the boys, her eyes would.

"Who was it, Katie?" Mary tried to sit up, but groaned.

"Easy, sister." She helped her lie down again. "It was Willis."

"Mark's Willis?"

"The same." She smiled a little. "He's home, and getting baptized, as you said he was going to do."

"You should trust me more often, shouldn't you?" Mary laughed once she was lying down again.

"I guess so." Once her sister was situated, she picked up the bible again.

"Has he changed much?" The topic turned right back to Willis.

"Not so much physically. Mentally, I really think he has." Katie sat back down on the chair. "He didn't question why I was going to be baptized once; he used to question it all the time when we were younger." She smiled a little.

"Katie, are you in love?" The tone she used made her skin crawl. It felt like Mary was upset with her for almost moving on.

"Why would you say that?"

"You're blushing." Mary teased her now. "Come on, admit it. You like Willis."

"Do not." She felt a blush growing on her cheeks. "Do you want me to keep reading Leviticus or do you want some food?"

"Lunch sounds great, actually, Katie." Her sister smiled. "Do you know if mom has made any yet?"

"No, but I can go check. I might get roped into helping cook lunch, so I might be a while if she hasn't made it."

"I'll take a nap, then." She rested her head back on the pillows, letting it roll to the side. Her eyes closed, and Katie brushed some hair out of her face. She set the bible on the nightstand, and then began to walk downstairs.

The stairs creaked and refused to stay quiet. For Mary's sake, she hoped she was a heavy sleeper.

Once she was at the bottom of the stairs, Katie walked into the large summer kitchen. Her mom sat on a stool, canning a quart or so of ripe peaches.

"Mary's wondering about lunch, mom."

"You can make her something, Katie." Her mother didn't look up from canning. "Your father is out butchering the pig, and your grandparents are on the porch. See if they'd like any food. Your younger brothers and sister will be coming in with more peaches soon."

"Of course, mother." She smiled, and began to walk towards the porch. The large house made it a long walk. As she walked, she admired the well-made furniture. Her dad had made most of it by hand before she was born.

She opened the door to the porch and saw her grandmother and grandfather sitting on the bench.

"Grandma, grandpa, would you like some lunch?"

"That sounds wonderful, Katie." Her grandfather smiled, and her grandmother nodded. "Is it ready?"

"Not yet. I'll come get you when it is, though, grandpa." With that, she smiled. In this area of Pennsylvania, potatoes grew well. She decided to make a potato salad for the family, and began to gather potatoes to boil. Her mother had passed the recipe down to her last year, and the only way she would ever remember it was to make it often.

As she began to fill a pot with water, she thought about what Mary was doing. Her tone had become bitter at the end of the conversation they'd had, and she had felt rather uncomfortable. Why would Mary be so bitter?

Willis was two years older than she was. He'd often brushed her aside, not intentionally, but brushed aside all the same. As far as Katie was aware, Mary didn't even like Willis.

She sighed softly and turned the faucet off. The community here had gotten running water a few years ago, and it was such a relief. No longer did they have to warm the bath water by the stove or run outside to the pump every time they wanted water. They still used the pump, of course, to get water for the animals, but for them, they used the tap.

She set the pot of potatoes to boil as she heard the door open again. In came the rest of her siblings: Wayne, John, Samuel, and Hannah. Hannah was the youngest; at the tender age of 5, she could carry but only two peaches.

"Come here, Hannah." She smiled, and held her hands out for the peaches. Katie decided that a peach cobbler could make Mary feel a little better. "Wayne, how many peaches in that bucket?"

"Close to a hundred. How many more do you need?" Wayne was the eldest of the children, and had yet to marry. There were rumors that he was seeing a woman of 22 at the Sunday singings by the name Mary (no relation to his sister).

"Hannah's going to give me her two, so probably six or seven." As she spoke, she took the two peaches from her sister's hands gently. Wayne nodded and set the peaches on the counter.

"Peach cobbler sounds wonderful, Katie." He smiled at her before taking the rest of his peaches to the summer kitchen. Samuel and John followed suit, but did not stop to give her peaches. Hannah simply requested to mash the peaches; gladly, she peeled the peaches and put them in a bowl.

Then, she gave the bowl and a thick wooden dowel to Hannah.

"Mash away." She smiled and let her sister mash the peaches. Then, she checked on the potatoes for the salad. When they were soft, she pulled them out of the pot and began to mash them for the salad.

In all, it took her an hour to make the potato salad and stick the cobbler in the oven. She called everyone else into the kitchen and then put some on a plate for Mary.

"I'll take some up to Mary. Mom, the cobbler has about half an hour; could you pull it out when it's done?"

"I got it, Katie." John spoke up. "You take care of Mary." John was a year away from his *rumspringa*, but he had this certain quality of stubbornness. She doubted he'd be gone for long.

"Thank you." She smiled. "Tell grandma and grandpa I'm upstairs, please."

"Of course." With that, she walked two plates of potato salad up to Mary's room. Well, Mary shared it with her and Hannah. The three beds stretched east to west across the room, with a small closet to the other end of the beds. A nightstand was situated to the left of each bed for braiding strings and bibles. Flowers sometimes made it in, but that was rare.

"Mary?" Katie gently shook her sister awake. "Lunch is ready." She set one plate on the nightstand by her bed, and then she walked to hers.

"Mmm?" Mary never woke well, but today was a different story. "You made potato salad?"

"Yeah. Our potatoes haven't been stored right, so they were beginning to go bad." She began to eat her food. "There's a peach cobbler in the oven."

"Fresh peaches?"

"Yes, Mary. With fresh peaches; freshly picked this afternoon, actually."

"I guess that's what the others have been doing."

"Mom's been canning all morning, but yes. Our brothers and Hannah have been picking peaches all morning, they told me." She smiled, and watched as Mary ate her lunch in silence. The silence hurt a little bit; they were a tightly-knit community. What could be causing her to stop talking to her own sister? "Mary, did I do something wrong?"

"What do you mean?"

"You've hardly spoken a word to me other than to confirm your thoughts." She took another bite of her salad. "Did I do something wrong?"

"No. I'm very happy for you." There was a bitter tone. "Cross my heart."

"Alright..." Katie wasn't convinced, but let the topic drop. She finished her potato salad, and gathered up her dishes to take downstairs. "Are you done, Mary?"

"Yes." She almost shoved the plate at her, hardly touched. "I lost my appetite."

"Do you want some peach cobbler when it finishes?"

"No." Mary rolled over. "I'm going to finish my nap."

Katie didn't have time to object before Mary seemed to completely ignore her. She sighed softly and began to walk back downstairs. Maybe she could can some peaches before her cobbler finished.

She washed the dishes and put them away in silence. Tomorrow was Sunday; would she miss visiting and singing to take care of her sister?

Her mom came in as she was drying the plates, and picked up the utensils to dry.

"Do you want to go to the evening singing tomorrow night, Katie?" Her mom's question was a little on the nose. She nodded slowly. "Have you talked to Mary about it?"

"Mary won't talk to me." She tried not to cry. "She won't tolerate me for more than a few minutes at a time before she slips back into silence."

"When did this start?"

"This afternoon, after Willis visited." A tear trickled down her cheek, and she almost dropped the plates. Her mother took the plates and rag from her, setting them on the counter. Instead of wiping her tears away, she hugged her. Katie couldn't remember the last time her mother hugged her.

"It'll be alright, Katie. I think she's upset she can't go out into the world yet. She wants to spread her wings as badly as you did." Her mother rubbed her back as she found herself crying. "I know you haven't seen her in two years; it's natural to feel like there's a gap there."

She sniffled, eventually calming down.

"Thanks mom."

"Now, I think you should get the cobbler out. Enjoy a big piece." Her mother pulled away. "I'll finish the dishes."

She managed a smile and pulled the cobbler out. It was a little burnt on the edges, but her mother had saved it from burning too much by turning the oven off. Now, she set it on the cool counter on top of a small washcloth. Then, she began to cut the pieces. She cut it so that everyone could have a piece, though she cut Hannah's a little smaller so hers could be a little bigger.

Her mother laughed, but knew that's how they all did it. Whoever made the cobbler got the largest piece since Hannah was too young to have a normal sized piece yet. She managed a smile, and scooped a piece up for Mary. She carried it up the stairs, and then set it on Mary's nightstand. Even if she didn't want it now, she would have a piece available for her.

Then, she walked back downstairs to enjoy her piece. The rest of the family was coming in, and they all took a piece. They left the largest piece for her, an unspoken rule in the house.

"Thanks, Katie." Her grandmother smiled. "You're wonderful."

They ate the cobbler in silence. Her mind reeled, but she couldn't turn off the thoughts that her sister was bitter over Willis' attention to her.

***

Katie smiled as she put on her best clothes for the singing. It was almost six PM on Sunday evening, and her mother was going to help Mary for the night. Wayne and John were old enough to go to the singing events as well. Their grandparents would entertain Hannah and Samuel for the night.

"Are you ready, Katie?" Wayne called from the room across the hall.

"Almost, Wayne! I'll meet you at the door."

"Okay." Her brother left her alone and let her get ready in piece. She pulled her hair into a braid and quickly tied it off. She'd had enough of her hair being in her face, the stringy ends particularly.

Then, she walked downstairs. In her blue dress with long sleeves, slightly lower neckline but still appropriate, she felt as if she were going to catch Willis' attention again. Maybe it wouldn't be so bad, to have

Willis paying attention to her. She did like him quite a bit, but wasn't sure she would like to marry him.

Based on their interactions earlier, however, she knew that it'd be a good choice to marry him. He'd blossomed into a young Amish man that no woman would be able to say no to.

With that thought tucked away in her head, she arrived at the door. Wayne and John were already there, both dressed in their best clothes. Their mother waited to see them off.

"I'll take good care of Mary tonight, Katie. Enjoy your night." Her words made Katie smile. "If she wants you here, I'll come get you, but I hope you get to enjoy the night." With that, she sent them off towards the barn where Sunday evening singing was held every week.

It was a silent, ten minute walk. The silence was not like those that Mary forced upon her. Instead, the silence filled her with hope and joy; this would be quite an exciting night. She would have a chance to see other members of the community that she hadn't seen, and possibly find someone who struck her fancy.

When they arrived at the barn, the singing was up and running already. She separated from her brothers, promising to find them at the end of the event. They smiled, nodded, and agreed to it. Then, they proceeded to join in on the festivities. A long table with food sat to one side of the barn.

She migrated over to see if someone had brought cherry cobbler. While her family didn't grow cherries, plenty of other families did. The table had plenty of finger foods, and two cherry cobblers sat to one side. One had already been half eaten, and the other was untouched. She cut herself a small slice of cherry cobbler and began to eat it.

"Katie?" A voice behind her made her jump; she almost lost her cherry cobbler. She turned around, and laid eyes on Willis.

"Willis." She smiled after swallowing. "I didn't expect to see you here today."

"I could say the same thing about you." He smiled back. "Is Mary doing better?"

"Mom's watching her tonight so I could come here. If I'm needed at home, someone else will come to get me." She smiled a little more. "Your baptism was a lovely service."

"Thank you." He couldn't help but grin at her with his goofy, toothy smile. "I hope your baptism service is as lovely." She felt her cheeks heating up a little.

"Is there a reason you wanted to talk to me, Willis?" She took another bite of her cherry cobbler. Cherry juices ran down her chin, and she managed to catch them with a napkin.

"Would you like to meet up next week at the evening singing?" He handed her another napkin as he asked. She almost choked on her cobbler.

"M-Me?" She couldn't believe his words. "You want to meet up with me next week?"

"Yes." His smile turned into a slight frown. "Do you not want to?"

"N-No, I want to." She managed another smile. "I didn't think you'd ask so soon."

"Wonderful!" He smiled, a little too excited. "I hope you don't mind that it was so soon."

"No, not at all." Her voice quivered a little. "I'm worried about how Mary will react, though." Willis' brows furrowed. "Mary's been giving me the silent treatment."

"Why?"

"I don't know." She sighed, and picked a plate up to set her cobbler on. "I think it has to do with your visit yesterday. It didn't start until after you visited."

"I only visited to say hello." His brows stayed furrowed. "I didn't mean to make her think I was interested in anyone unwillingly..."

"She teased me about it before we went on *rumspringa*. Now, she teases with a bitter tone and a scornful eye." She sighed, dabbing at her cherry stained lips. "She won't even hold a conversation with me beyond making sure she knows what's going on."

"Do you think she wanted me?"

"I think it's because her *rumspringa* was delayed. She's a lot like you were before you left, Willis." She took another bite of her cobbler as the rest of the group started another song. "She wants to leave the community for good."

"I don't think she'll want to after she spends some time out in the real world." He cut himself a piece of cobbler as he spoke. "I thought I wanted to, and then I realized that it was nothing without the community. Without you." He flashed her a smile before he took a bite of his cobbler.

"Without me?" She found herself blushing again. The heat in her cheeks told her so.

He nodded slowly as he swallowed.

"Without you, I found that the women wanted to be with me. Apparently, I'm a good looker. Until they realize I won't be able to pay for everything they want, at least." He laughed. "All the girls I met wanted money."

"A lot of guys I met simply wanted me on their arm for a pretty face." She sighed, rolling her eyes. "I hated it. Eventually, I gave up and started saying no to them. One of them had ties to a gang, and...and they almost killed me. That's why I came home." In the middle of her story, her tone changed. She felt tears welling in her eyes, but she refused to cry.

"I'm sorry to hear that, Katie." Willis put a hand on her shoulder softly. "I think it was smart to come back home after that."

"Mary broke her leg the next week, and we had to postpone my baptism." She pushed tears out of her eyes softly, trying not to make it obvious that she wanted to cry.

"Katie?" A voice interrupted the conversation. "Mary's asking for you at home." Looking around, she found Samuel standing in front of her. "Mom sent me."

"Thanks, Samuel. I'll walk you home." She cut another piece of cherry cobbler before she turned to Willis. "I'll see you around, Willis."

"See you around, Katie." He smiled at her, and gave her a small wink before she led her younger brother out of the room. "I'll tell your brothers that you had to go early." She smiled.

"Thanks." With that, they left the singing and began to walk back to their home.

"Can I have a bite, Katie?"

"That's why I cut another piece, Sam." She smiled, and used a fork to cut a small bite off for her brother. "Here you go."

"Thanks!" Her brother's face lit up, and she couldn't help but smile as he took a bite of the cobbler. "Cherry?"

"Yes. I don't know who made it, but it's good, isn't it?" She took another bite after she finished speaking.

"Yes." Her brother smiled. "Are you okay?"

"Willis and I were having a conversation about our time outside the community."

"Oh. Is it hard for you to talk about?"

"At times." She smiled a little. "Tonight was one of those times, but it had nothing to do with you or Willis."

"Did you enjoy the time with Willis?"

"Yes." She smiled, brushing a loose strand of her hair behind her ear. "I did."

"Should we expect a wedding soon?" Samuel began to tease her. "Willis and Katie getting married?"

"Samuel!" She half-scolded him, but the laugh in her voice gave her away. "I don't know." She sighed. "I honestly don't know. You know relationships are never public until a wedding date is for sure."

"I know." He sighed now. "Can I have another piece?"

"Fork?" She held her hand out for his fork as they neared the porch of their house. He happily handed her the fork, and she gave him another piece. "Thank you, Katie."

"You're welcome. Share the rest of that piece with mom and Hannah, okay?"

"Okay!" He took the plate and forks before heading towards their parents' bedroom.

"And with dad if he's home." She called after him, and only got a thumbs-up in the air. She laughed, and then headed upstairs to her room. Mary was fast asleep in her bed. As quietly as she could, she changed into something she could sleep in. Hannah was not asleep yet.

"Katie, is that you?" Mary softly spoke.

"Yes. Did I wake you?"

"No." She rolled away from her. "You can go back to the singing."

"But Sam said..." She was unsure of what to do; now half changed into something to sleep in, she couldn't go back.

"Mom had to go do something; I'm fine." The bitter tone returned. "Go away."

"Mary, we have to talk about this." She pulled her sleeping clothes on the rest of the way and sat down at the head of Mary's bed. "Why are you being so bitter?"

"Did Willis ask you to meet him next week?"

"What?"

"Did Willis ask you to meet him next week?" Her sister repeated the question, but didn't look at her.

"Yes." She softly answered. "But he didn't mean to upset you yesterday."

"I thought you were going to wait until I was out to do that!" Mary almost exploded at her.

"What?"

"I thought you were going to wait until I was in the world to do that." She sniffled. "No one ever seems to care what I think!"

"Mary, that's not true, and you know it." She touched her sister's shoulder. "What do you think?"

"I want to go out." Her sister's voice quivered. "I want to be independent." At this, Katie crossed the room to face her sister. Tears streamed down her cheeks, and she was sobbing too hard to say anything.

Katie simply hugged her tightly, unsure of how to take the new development. However, the hug didn't last long. Mary pushed her away hard, sending her to the floor. She sat up slowly, her head spinning lightly.

"What was that for?" She tried not to sound upset with her sister, but failed.

"Hugging me!" Mary now yelled at her. "I don't like being touched."

"I'm sorry. I thought you could use a hug." She sincerely apologized. "Are you okay?"

"What?"

"Are you okay, Mary?" She sat on her knees, closer to the bed. "Emotionally, are you okay?"

Her sister sniffled, confused by the question. She let her sister take her time, hoping that their parents hadn't heard Mary yelling.

"I-I...I'm okay now." She sniffled again, wiping her eyes. "Do you think you'll marry him, Katie?"

"I don't know." She smiled a little. "Please, don't tell anyone."

"I won't." Her sister sniffled again. She handed her a napkin, and waited as Mary blew her nose. "I think you two make a good couple."

"Are you done ignoring me?"

"Ignoring you?"

"You weren't doing it on purpose?"

"No. I wasn't sure why you were the one watching me so often." Her sister propped herself up on her elbow, careful of putting extra weight on her broken leg.

"Because I love you, Mary." She smiled softly. "Everyone else has been helping can."

"You don't really like to can, I remember now."

"Yup." She laughed a little as she remembered the incident that had turned her off of canning. Her finger had gotten stuck in a jar or a lid – she couldn't ever quite remember which – and had been covered by scalding fruit. Her finger was still scarred from it.

"I'm sorry, Katie." She spoke in a soft voice. "I didn't mean to tear you away from the singing."

"It's alright, Mary." She squeezed her sister's hand lightly before pulling away. "Why don't you get some rest?"

"The peach cobbler was delicious, by the way." Her sister smiled. "Thank you."

"You're welcome." She smiled. Maybe this would end well after all.

***

A month and a half later, Katie stood in her room, wearing a simple blue dress with a big bunch of flowers in her hands. The weekend after Willis had asked to see her the next week, he drove her home. Wayne and John left them alone to talk, having left earlier in the evening.

Willis had made the journey to his house at two in the morning, and their friendship acted as a catalyst. It was the quickest courtship they had seen in the community in decades, her grandmother said.

"Katie?" Hannah's voice filtered up the stairs. She turned around, and saw her youngest sibling sitting on the top stair. "You wove Willis?"

"Yes. I love Willis." She smiled, and picked up her younger sister. "One day, you too will be in love. It won't be for years, but it will be soon."

"Ew." She made a face. "Me no wove boys!" Katie laughed.

"Do you like my dress?" She quickly distracted her sister.

"I do!" She smiled widely. "Katie wook pretwy!" She laughed again.

"Do you want to wear a blue dress too, Hannah?" When her sister nodded excitedly, she set her down on the bed and looked for Hannah's blue dress. She found it under the bed, and helped her younger sister change.

Mary had left to explore the outside world the week before, but was returning to see her sister get married. She would be wearing something from the outside world – a dress, she believed it was, in a greenish color.

She shook her head lightly and began to braid Hannah's hair as she hummed a hymn. They still had about an hour before the wedding was to begin. They would make visits next weekend, since they had church tomorrow. Due to the timing of the year, they were able to get married quickly.

"Is Hannah up there with you, Katie?" Her mother's voice came up the stair case.

"Yes, mother." She smiled. "She's with me."

"Katie wook pwetty!" Her sister again complimented her, pronouncing the word 'pretty' differently than she had before. It was all part of a five year old's charm, though.

"Okay; I wanted to make sure she hadn't run off. Willis will be here soon; are you ready?"

"I'm ready. I didn't think he'd be here for another hour..."

"He's going to be early." Her mother did not hesitate to say it. "He told me last night that he wanted to see you before the wedding, but I asked him not to come so early."

"It's alright, mom. Is everyone else here?"

"Everyone's early, oddly enough. When he gets here, we can start." When she said that, her nerves began to jump. She was really doing this; she was really getting married.

The door downstairs opened, and she heard her to-be husband's voice in the hallway. She sent Hannah down ahead of her, her braid wildly flinging against the air as she ran. Katie took in a deep breath, and then began to walk downstairs.

The ceremony was all that she had hoped it would be. Mary had brought a friend with her – a guy who thought he was falling in love with her. They spent an entire afternoon singing, dancing, and enjoying the community's company. For the moment, they were to stay with her family until their new house was finished. The community was going to help them work on it tomorrow, so it shouldn't take long at all.

At the end of the festivities, Katie essentially collapsed in Willis' arms. Mary and her friend had driven home. Everyone else was getting ready to go; they had a long buggy ride ahead of them to get back to her place. Willis placed a soft kiss on her forehead before helping her up and out to the buggy.

"I love you." He spoke the words first. They had yet to say them to each other, but in the quiet of the night in the buggy, he broke the silence with them.

"I love you too, Willis." She couldn't help but feel an overwhelming smile on her face. A sense of belonging took over her, and she rested her head on his chest as they began the ride home. It was difficult to find a comfortable position in the bouncing buggy. Sleeping would have to wait until they arrived home.

"Are you looking forward to having a family?" He again spoke up.

"Yes." She couldn't stop her smile from widening. "I want to have a large family. Five kids, at least."

"Five kids, at least, it is." He smiled and laughed. "It sounds wonderful. And on our farm, what shall we grow?"

"Cherries, peaches, potatoes, and anything else you can think of." She smiled. "I can farm, and you can put your carpenter skills to good use."

"Good thing I have my own tools." Another chuckle came from his mouth. It shook his chest under her, and she smiled. The silence set in again, but it was a good, comfortable type. She bit her lip softly, and pressed her head against his shoulder. He put an arm around her, drawing her closer to him on the seat.

Before she could object, he had a blanket out from under the seat and laid it across the both of them.

"Better?" He smiled down at her.

"Much, thank you." She couldn't hide her smile, even if she wanted to. "Can I fall asleep now?"

"We're almost there, Katie." He brushed some of the loose hair out of her face. "But I will carry you in if you fall asleep."

"I love you so much." Her words echoed softly in the dark night, and she closed her eyes. His arms held her closer, and she could feel the buggy bounce up and down under them.

As she was falling asleep, the buggy came to a sudden, jerky stop. Willis stopped her from falling off the bench, and picked her up.

"But I'm not asleep..."

"I want to carry you in." He smiled down at her. "Sleep. We can always talk tomorrow. You're exhausted."

"Thank you." She smiled, speaking softly. He opened the door and walked her inside. She closed her eyes again, and found herself quickly drifting off to sleep. She felt him carry her up the stairs. He set her on the bed, and she heard him shuffling about the room for a few moments.

He got in bed beside her, and she felt a different kind of material touch her skin. He'd changed clothes before he got in with her. She smiled, and drifted off into a wonderful sleep.

Tears of an Amish Widow

Erica Hennig

There were a lot of things in life that Hannah King imagined she'd be. A mother, a wife, possibly even a mentor to young women; a widow was not something she'd imagined for herself.

There was an illness running through the little Plain community. It was something like pneumonia, but the English doctors were having a hard time controlling it as well. Hannah's husband, Joab, was a farmer with a caring heart. He chose to follow the doctor around and help him however he could. Since the illness was contagious, Joab eventually became sick.

Hannah wasn't going to let this illness stay in the community anymore. She made the decision to take Joab to the actual English hospital. Though they were able to keep him alive a little longer, they still could not save Joab. Hannah was crushed, her heart felt as though it had been ripped out of her chest and beaten with a sledgehammer over and over.

How am I going to take care of our little Samuel? How will I live? Who will take care of me?

The oncoming depression wasn't one she could push away with a few good thoughts and a well-placed Bible verse. She desperately tried praying, hoping that the God she served would send a sign that everything would be alright... but nothing came. No signs in the sky, no angels to comfort, and no one to care for her and her little boy.

Ultimately, she knew that the community would take care of her for a time, but she also knew that she would have to pull herself together eventually. Especially if she was going to continue to support her son. He no longer had a father, and Hannah was determined to make sure he had a mother.

Day in and day out, she began to do what she could to care for Samuel. She worked in the local store, and sold things she knitted at the market on the weekends. Hannah would help in the schoolhouse if they let her, and they did until Samuel got to be the age that he could go to school. The community leaders decided having one of the students' parents there would cause a conflict in the community as to why a certain parent was allowed there and none others.

Just as the new school year was around the corner, the school teacher—Miss Schwartz—got married and decided to quit teaching. Hannah didn't understand how the community could let something like that happen. She went on a rampage one day and told the leaders exactly what she thought of them in the little church building where they were meeting.

"How could you leave the children with no one? Who in this community will train our children on the right path? You must have *something* in place! Surely, you're not that stupid."

She heard a throat clear behind her and saw a handsome, young man standing in the doorway. He smiled as her face flushed with embarrassment.

"Ms. King, this is Michael Fisher," one of the elders said. "He will be the new school teacher. We have decided that you will assist him for the first three weeks of classes, then you must find something else to occupy your time."

"'Occupy my time?' You make teaching sound like a hobby! Isn't investing in the next generation important to you?" Hannah felt a hand on her shoulder and she knew it was the new guy, Michael. Something about his touch calmed her, and her heart instantly ached for the tender touch of a husband again.

"Ms. King," Michael's voice was barely above a whisper. "Let them do what they feel is right. I care about the children just as much as you do. We'll work something out for you."

Hannah relaxed a little, nodded in response, then turned around and walked out of the church. She discovered that the men in that room might not have cared for the children, but the man taking over as school teacher certainly did. And she could get behind a man that was confident in what he was doing. She was going to make the next three weeks the most meaningful yet.

Samuel was so excited for the first day of school that he could hardly contain himself. Hannah walked with him a little earlier than most other students. She wanted to be there early to make a better impression than the first time for Michael.

He probably won't even remember me anyway, she thought to herself. *Almost every single girl in the community has made contact with him. I'm sure we've all started to look the same to him.* Though Hannah was afraid to admit what exactly that meant, even to herself. She hated lumping herself in with all of the young, unmarried girls in the community, but sometimes she found herself acting just like them. Of course it was only a few years ago that she was unmarried and pining for every guy that walked into her life.

Her train of thought was interrupted by Samuel suddenly dashing off toward the school.

"Samuel, wait!"

Hannah tried to call him back or catch up with him, but he had such a head start that he was in the school building before she had even crested the hill the school was standing on. Michael popped his head out of the door, probably looking for the parents of the small child who had just entered the school an entire hour before school was even to start. As soon as he saw Hannah, he smiled wide.

"Ms. King," he declared instantly.

So much for forgetting who I am, she thought as her face grew warm.

"Mr. Fisher," she spoke politely. "I just want to apologize for the way we met—"

Michael held his hand up. "No need. All is forgiven. And please, call me Michael."

"Hannah." She stuck out her hand for him to shake, but he took it and kissed it lightly instead. Her heart skipped a beat.

"The pleasure is mine," he said as he looked into her eyes. His were a deep green that fit well with the sandy blond hair on his head and tan skin she could see. Hannah thought he looked almost too tan to be a teacher, but decided the first official meeting wasn't the right time to bring that up.

"Samuel and I are here early to help you set up since it's the first day of school," Hannah quickly changed the subject before her mind went any further away from the original reason she was there so early.

Michael turned and walked into the building, ready to have a helper there.

"I'm glad you'll be here for a few weeks. Sometimes the first three weeks are the hardest on a teacher."

"You've taught before?" Samuel sounded surprised. Michael laughed.

"Of course, buddy," Michael bent down to Samuel's level and addressed him directly. "I was a teacher in another community before I came here."

"Why didn't you stay there then?"

"Because I heard there was another town that needed help, and I like a good hero story." Michael winked as Samuel's eyes grew wide.

Hannah laughed at the exchange before telling Samuel to make sure that every desk had pencils.

As the boy ran off, Hannah began to explain to Michael what they had done last year before Michael cut her off with a wave of his hand.

"I do appreciate the input Hannah, but I would like to do something a little different this time. The children don't know me, and I don't know any of them. I don't want to really come down as an overbearing teacher on my first day." Michael winked. Hannah didn't understand that logic, and she certainly didn't appreciate feeling like she was being spoken to condescendingly.

"Excuse me, sir, but I think we should at least address what the children did." Hannah was going to let him have it anyway. "The children come here to learn, not to make friends with the teacher. If you think for one second I'll let you get away with talking to me like that, you have some life choices to reevaluate." Michael's eyebrows shot up, but he didn't say anything.

Hannah continued. "You might think you're some big hot shot coming here on the invitation of the elders, but you're only here because I already have a child and they won't let parents of a child in the school be the teacher. So you can take the smug, entitled attitude and stick it... somewhere!" She turned and walked out of the building, now feeling like a bit of a moron for telling the handsome, new school teacher off. She was only outside a few minutes before Samuel came and got her.

"Mama, don't let Mr. Fisher scare you away," he spoke tenderly to her. "Besides, maybe he can help you become an even better hero." Hannah looked at her son and realized that even though she didn't think very highly of herself, he thought the world of her. And she wasn't going to let him down; not today, and not ever.

"Okay," she consented as she gave Samuel a hug. "Let's go inside and show him how it's done."

The next few week flew by quickly, and the fact that Michael had been making subtle advances wasn't lost on Hannah. She loved the fact that someone was even toying with the idea of courting her. Since it had been almost five years since Joab had passed on, Hannah didn't think any man would ever take a liking to a woman with a child.

There was only a small problem with the whole situation, and Hannah hated to admit it to herself. Abigail Miller had also shown an interest in the young Mr. Fisher. She was by far the prettiest girl in town with her beautiful blonde hair, deep blue eyes and nearly flawless skin. There wasn't much wrong with Abigail, except that if she didn't get her way she tended to have a fit. But with all of the guys in town constantly pining for her, that rarely happened. Until Michael Fisher came along.

Hannah wasn't sure if he was declining young Abigail's advances or simply playing hard to get, but it made Hannah a little nervous. She felt like there might have been something between them, but this was the last day that she would see Michael on a regular basis. Since it wasn't out of the realm of normal things she would do, she had already decided that she would walk Samuel home from school everyday. Especially if that meant she got to see Michael Fisher for a few minutes.

As all of the children were released to go home, Hannah decided to see if she could get an idea of what was going on in his head.

"This is my last day," she picked up a pencil off the floor as if it was the only purpose she had in the world. She looked up at Michael at the front of the room. He simply nodded, his face tight with emotion.

"Are you okay?" Suddenly nothing else mattered. She moved to the front of the room and stood next to him.

"I just hate it that things have to come to an end," he began to cry. Hannah was shocked. She'd never really seen a grown man cry before, and she wasn't sure what to do. She put her hand on his arm.

"How can I help you?"

"You can stay," he chuckled. They both knew that wasn't her decision and she said as much. Michael replied, "That doesn't mean you can't try to get an extension."

"I'm a woman," Hannah shot back. "They are far less likely to listen to me than they are to you. Besides, you're the teacher. You know what you need far better than I do."

"All I need is you."

Hannah froze. Did she just hear him correctly? "What?"

He pulled away. "You're right, I shouldn't have said that. I apologize." He began busying himself with unnecessary papers on the desk.

"Michael." Hannah grabbed his arm and he stopped. He looked at her and their eyes met. Tears were brimming in his eyes. She wanted to hear him say it again. "What did you say?"

"All I need is you." He turned to face her fully. Her heartbeat sped up, but her breathing became shallow. She knew this feeling; Joab used to make her feel this way. But Joab was gone, so she attempted to push all thoughts of her dead husband out of her mind.

Michael looked at her a moment longer, but he must have seen the inner turmoil because he finally said, "No." And he turned and went back to the useless straightening.

"Did I do something wrong?" Hannah's heart hurt a little as she was suddenly treated very coldly. He stopped.

"No, but I need to take this slowly. Not for your sake, but for mine. There's so much I haven't been able to tell you because we've been at school. Let's have dinner tonight. Bring Samuel. The Miller's live right next door and they have a son he can play with."

Hannah knew the Miller's well, especially because Abigail was the one after Michael's heart. This was a good sign though, because it meant that although Abigail was trying, she wasn't doing as well as she might have thought. And she wasn't asked over for dinner like Hannah. She would still be careful not to give in too much to this. There had been too many times already where men thought they wanted Hannah, but they didn't want Samuel. Since the pair were a package deal, there wasn't much option once they realized how serious Hannah was about her son.

I guess we'll find out tonight how he really feels.

As he usually was, Samuel was ecstatic to be spending any time with Mr. Fisher.

"Do we need to bring anything, Mama? I can't imagine that a *man* would cook anything well." Samuel made a face as he finished his thought. Hannah laughed.

"Samuel, don't be so mean," she playfully scolded him. "Maybe he had all sisters and learned how to cook from them. Maybe he was an only child. I don't know, but you can ask him when we get there."

The ten-minute walk seemed to be the longest walk of their lives. As they got closer, Samuel got more talkative, but Hannah became more quiet. *What if he decides he doesn't like me? How will I tell Samuel?*

Does he even like Samuel? It seems as though he likes children, but sometimes Samuel is a handful. Maybe we should turn around...

The doubting game was becoming too much. Hannah felt a hand wrap around her hand and looked down to find her son had grasped her and was smiling up at her.

"Remember Mama," Samuel said sweetly. "No matter what this man thinks of you, I still love you." She felt an unchecked tear slide down her cheek. She stopped and scooped the little boy into her arms, as they held each other and cried. When Hannah finally put Samuel down he said, "Besides, Jesus still loves you too. And He's the only man you need that *really* matters."

Hannah had to keep from crying because they had already rounded the corner onto the street where Michael lived and he was standing in the doorway waiting for them. Hannah began to apologize for keeping him waiting, but he just waved his hand as he usually did when he didn't want to hear excuses.

"Anything you need to say isn't going to make up for the lost time, so let's not waste any more with apologies." He smiled as if to say there was no need to feel bad for anything she did, though she still felt the need to apologize for apologizing before realizing that would have been counterproductive. She stepped over the threshhold behind her son and was surprised to see an almost immaculate house with the smell of roast beef, carrots and potatoes wafting throughout.

"Mama, it doesn't smell this good when you cook!" Samuel seemed to suddenly have no filter. Thankfully, Michael took it gracefully and defended Hannah's honor.

"Now now, that's not what we say to our mother, is it?" He knelt to Samuel's level, ever the teacher. "She cooks for you, doesn't she?"

The little boy nodded.

"You're never hungry, are you?"

He shook his head.

"Do you sleep in a house?"

A nod.

"Do you have decent clothes to wear?"

Another nod.

"How about some nice shoes?"

One more nod for good measure.

"Then you only say nice things about the woman that treats you well."

"Yes sir," Samuel said before Michael nodded and stood.

"Now," he clapped his hands together. "Who's ready for dinner?"

During dinner, Samuel asked every question he said he was going to, from how he knows how to cook to why is his house so clean to why does he teach. Everything seemed to be going really well until suddenly the 5-year-old had a different plan for the interrogation.

"Do you plan on marrying Mama?"

Hannah's face quickly grew warm and she studied the plate in front of her, afraid of what Michael would say. *This wasn't supposed to happen!*

Without skipping a beat, Michael replied, "Well, that really depends on her. I've already made my decision, but if she keeps pushing me away... then we'll see."

"That would be really stinky. Because Mama really likes you and she's a lot happier with you in her life. In fact, I don't think I've ever seen her this happy. She even sings in her sleep now." Michael laughed at the boy's sudden burst of random facts.

"Oh, does she?" Samuel wasn't even phased.

"Yeah. I think they're songs she used to sing with Papa, but I was a baby when he died, so I only hear stories now. But I think she told me once that was a song she used to sing with him." Samuel shrugged before adding, "Do you have anything for dessert?"

"As a matter of fact I do. Then, you should go play with David Miller next door while you Mama and I talk about grown up stuff."

Samuel seemed to like that idea, so Michael went to get the dessert. Strawberry shortcake with vanilla ice cream.

"Where did you learn how to make ice cream?" Hannah tried to keep the conversation away from their relationship for the time being. She was still reeling from the question of marriage.

"Oh that's simple stuff really... I just went to the English store in town." They all laughed. "More accurately, I have a Mennonite friend who gives me ice cream on a regular basis. It's a treat for me and not one I share with everyone. Tonight, I have two honored guests in my home and I want you both to know that you're special to me."

It was quiet for a few moments, but finally Samuel pushed his chair back and got up from the table without asking.

"I think that was my cue to leave." With that, he walked out the front door and closed it behind him.

"I can't argue with his logic, even if he didn't ask to be excused." Michael looked at Hannah and began his thought. "I've been meaning to tell you this since I met you, but I really do have intentions of marrying you... but like I told Samuel, that is entirely up to you." He sighed and leaned back in his chair. "Would you like to move to the living room? The dishes can wait until later."

Hannah was so enamored by the way Michael's house looked that she couldn't imagine that he was actually fine with leaving dishes unwashed, but she didn't argue because she knew this was a conversation they needed to have.

Once they sat down and were comfortable, Michael continued his thought.

"There is no one in this world who has made me feel more comfortable than you have. From the second I heard how passionate you were about the children until I saw you and Samuel walking up to my house with red eyes from crying, and right up until this moment; there is no one in the world I want in my life more than you and Samuel." He smiled when he said her son's name.

"Who named him?" Michael asked.

"Joab did. He was sick when Samuel was born and said that I was to dedicate him to the Lord just like Hannah did in the Bible."

"Were you having trouble conceiving as well? Actually, I'm sorry—"

Hannah laughed. "No apologies needed, and no we weren't. But he knew from the start that he probably wasn't going to make it. In some ways, it made his passing easier, but in others... it just became harder."

They were quiet for a few minutes before Michael reached out and grabbed Hannah's hand in both of his.

"No matter what anyone says or what anyone does, I will always be here and I will always make my way back to you if you ever feel like we're too far apart."

Hannah had tears in her eyes and she didn't know what to think. The only thing she could manage to get out was, "Why me?"

Michael smiled.

"Because you're everything I've asked God for in a wife, and Samuel is everything I ever wanted in a son."

"What about Abigail Miller? I thought she was interested in you." Hannah simply had to know. She didn't want there to be anymore confusion or dissension between her and the Miller's.

Michael simply shook his head. "She's okay as a person and very beautiful. But she's no Hannah King. You tend to doubt yourself, but you're more beautiful than ten Abigail Millers'. You have beautiful brown hair that reminds me of dark chocolate and rich brown eyes to match. You have cute freckles on your nose that almost seem to contract when you squint your eyes just right... and when you get embarrassed or upset, your face gets really red and it's actually kind of cute." He winked at her.

Despite the tears, she managed to laugh at the last part. She didn't know if she should be rejoicing for herself or praying for Abigail. She loved Abigail like a little sister and would rather have her happy. As if

Michael could suddenly read her mind, he pulled his hands away and gave an exasperated sigh.

"Hannah, Hannah. Why can't you just take the gift that God is giving you? Stop pushing His free love away and stop pushing me away. I'm not usually one to give ultimatums, but if you can't make up your mind, then maybe we shouldn't even try." With that, Michael stood up and went to the kitchen to finish washing the dishes. As he left the living room he called back, "When you're done in there, go ahead and let yourself out. Thank you for coming over."

It was at that moment that Hannah realized she had just potentially thrown her life away. She couldn't move from her spot as much as she didn't want to be there anymore, but she had to do something. So she got down on her knees and just began crying out to the Lord for all of the things she had done to push the people in her life away. She had never done this before, and it was weird to do it in a place that wasn't even familiar, but she knew she needed to do it and she didn't care who could see her.

She didn't know how long she was there for, but when she opened up her eyes and wiped the tears away, she noticed that both Samuel and Michael were on their faces as well, crying and praying along with her. Michael was closest to her, so she put her hand on his back. He began to shake and sob even louder.

When he finally quieted down, she put her mouth down by his ear and whispered, "All I want is you, Michael. I give myself to you."

He breathed a heavy sigh and finally forced himself up. They looked into each other's eyes and knew this was only the beginning of something much deeper than either of them could fathom. He smiled a crooked smile as Samuel sat up with tears still streaming down his face.

"Geez, if you wanted a revival meeting, why didn't you just set one up with the elders?"

Two days later was Sunday, and the town went to church as usual. Michael grabbed Hannah and Samuel on their way out and asked them to stay a few more minutes with him.

"I have something I want to say to the elders and I want you to be there when I do."

"Both of us?" Hannah asked curiously.

"Of course. You come as the whole package." He smiled at them and Samuel couldn't contain his excitement over the mysterious way Michael was acting.

As soon as the last of the churchgoers had left and there were only the elders and the trio, Michael made his move.

"Excuse me, I have something I would like to propose."

The elders looked at him curiously and the preacher said, "Go on."

"I would like for Hannah to be my assistant for the rest of the school year. I know you told her that she couldn't, but the rule that she would be partial to her son is a little silly, since I've seen her in action and she's only more strict on him. These last three weeks have been a huge transition into a position I've never really had before, and Hannah has made everything I've done seem like it was extremely easy."

"We will consider your request, but we can't make any promises," the preacher seemed to be the speaker of the elders today.

"There's also another thing that you might want to consider," Michael seemed to be struggling with this one a little more. He looked at Hannah for just a moment and she nodded, not knowing what he was going to say but showing her support in whatever was about to happen.

"I want to marry her too."

The elders went into a tizzy trying to wrap their heads around this proclamation.

"What? You want to marry a widow?"

"What about children of your own?"

"What about Abigail Miller? Surely she's the better fit."

All of these quick suggestions cut Hannah's heart like a knife, but Michael stopped them all with a wave of his hand.

"My mind's been made up. I love Hannah King and have since I watched her stand up to you almost four weeks ago. And I love Samuel. He's dedicated his life for God's use only and he's everything I always prayed I would have in a son. As for Abigail, God will give her the right man at the right time. I'm not that man, and this is not that time."

The elders simply couldn't believe what they were hearing, but suddenly decided they needed to act right then. They quickly shuffled out of the sanctuary into a back room to discuss, leaving Michael, Hannah, and Samuel alone.

Hannah started to feel those doubts come in again, but this time she stopped them before they could start. *I have a man for the first time in years that loves me like God loves me! How can I ever say no to that kind of love?*

Samuel was starting to get anxious, but Michael wouldn't let him leave, so they began playing a game of tag in the sanctuary. Hannah sat and watched them play, laughing at the way Michael looked, behaving like a 5-year-old.

After almost an hour, the elders finally emerged from the back room. Some of them looked overjoyed and others looked pensive. Hannah wasn't sure if that was a good sign, but she braced her heart for anything.

"Don't." Michael had come up behind her and must have seen her body language. "Don't close your heart. Open it up. Allow yourself to feel. How can you love if you don't let yourself get hurt once in awhile?"

Hannah wasn't sure how to answer that question, but she didn't have the time. Samuel abruptly stopped gallivanting and returned to his place by his mother's side.

The preacher spoke. "We have considered your requests and have but one condition." He looked at the three of them equally. "That you must stay in this town for the rest of your lives and give your lives to serving the children of this community. They need people with big hearts like yours, and this town needs people with new hope to bring a fresh perspective."

"Wait, I have to stay here for the rest of my life?" Samuel asked. "Can't I go home?"

They all laughed as Michael explained he had to stay in the town, not in the church itself. "Ooohhh. Cool!"

Hannah was in shock that they were actually letting this happen. "You're okay with us getting married?"

"God has ordained every man, a wife." The preacher submitted. "And God has ordained every woman, a husband. You have been blessed enough to have been ordained two husbands. The favor of God is on your life, child. We know you won't do anything that would hurt us with it."

Michael pulled her into a hug, as he was still in shock that they said yes. He began to cry into her hair as she cried into his chest. They were going to get to start fresh on everything. And it was the best feeling ever.

Abigail still came to the school everyday to see Michael. Maybe she was hoping she could change his mind, because by now the whole town knew that Michael and Hannah were courting to be married. By the end of that first week, Hannah finally pulled Abigail aside and asked her what was going on.

"I just can't believe that a handsome man like Michael would fall for a widow like you."

Hannah did all she could not to choke the woman out with a bunch of children still around. She wanted to be a good example.

"Well, my dear, I'm sorry that you didn't get your way this time. I guess when it comes to matters of the heart, you're just not the expert."

Abigail huffed, "Who made you the judge on what I'm expert in?"

"Well I know good wife material when I see it, honey. If you want I can help you hone that passion a little better so that people start to take you more seriously. Men like a woman that can really stand up for herself without looking like a 5-year-old."

Abigail looked as if she'd been accosted, but she gathered her composure enough to curtly say, "Maybe I would like that."

Hannah smiled, hoping for only the best in this situation. "Alright then. I'll see you tonight at my house."

"Tonight?"

"Yes. If you want a husband, we must start right away."

"No, I can't do tonight! I have plans."

"With?"

Abigail suddenly looked very flustered. "Someone."

Hannah's eyebrows shot up. "A boy?"

"It's none of your business!" And she picked up the dress from around her heels and marched down the hill.

"What was that all about?" Michael asked as Hannah came back in to finish getting the room ready for tomorrow.

"Abigail's been seeing someone, but she's been coming up here everyday for you. I was nice, but I basically told her she needed to stop."

"I never heard you use those words. It actually sounded as if you were genuinely interested in her life."

Hannah smiled. "It's not like I'm not. I still want to see her do well, even though in her eyes I stole the man she wanted."

Michael stopped what he was doing and pulled her into him. "Hey." He looked deep into her eyes until it felt like he was seeing into her soul.

"No one stole me from anyone. I am my own person and I make my own decisions. Take those thoughts out of your mind right now."

Hannah closed her eyes to clear her head. Suddenly she felt something on her lips. She opened her eyes and saw that Michael was kissing her! She instinctively pulled back and it shocked him.

"What's wrong?"

"Let's... do that again."

This time she was prepared. And it was a glorious kiss with so much emotion and passion behind it. Hannah wasn't sure what had happened last Friday when they were on the floor of his living room, but since then their relationship seemed to be on a fast-track. It was overwhelming at times, but in times like this it felt just right. This was the healing that she needed after Joab died.

As Michael pulled away from Hannah and they looked at each other again, she told him, "Just now was the first time I've thought of Joab in a longing way in a week. Should I feel bad about that?"

Michael shook his head. "The memories of those we loved will always be there, but we have to learn to move on. Thinking of Joab in a longing way meant that even while I was trying to make a move, you were shutting me out. And you did. Now that you've experienced some healing and given a lot of that hurt to God, there's room in your heart to love again."

He suddenly became very serious as he got down on one knee and pulled a small box out of his pocket. He opened it as he spoke to reveal a gold ring with a small diamond set in it.

"With this ring I want you to promise me that you will always be open and vulnerable to me about what's going on. That you will tell me when you're hurting and that you'll tell me when we can rejoice together."

She nodded, too overwhelmed to speak. Her vision became cloudy as he finished his speech.

"As I give you this ring, I promise that I will always protect you and lead you in the ways that God is showing me to take. I promise that I will love and care for Samuel as my own and that he will be my own son... just as you will be my own wife."

Hannah managed to squeak out a "yes" as she threw her arms around her beloved Michael and they cried.

"I love you, my crying widow." They both laughed through the tears as they knew this would certainly not be the last time they cried together.

Their foundation was built solidly on the passion of teaching children and leading each other into the deeper things of God. Hannah knew that this was the best way to start any marriage, and she was blessed to get a second chance to do it all again. This time, she knew it would be for eternity.

When Amish Love Finds A Way

Stephanie Swift

"Katherine, for the love of all things holy and good, will you please stop?"

Katherine Mills sat upright on the church pew and furrowed a brow at her younger brother, Jonah. The worship service would be starting soon, but she couldn't concentrate after discovering one of the buttons on Jonah's shirt was missing. She turned his wrist over to inspect the cuff...again.

"Why didn't you mention it this morning?" she whispered. "I could've mended it before we left."

Jonah jerked his arm from her grasp as his eyes roamed over the congregation. An elderly woman seated in front of them passed a snide glance their way, but the old gossipmonger was the least of her concern.

"Katherine, I'm not a kid anymore. It can wait. Now please stop embarrassing me."

Katherine laced her fingers together on top of her lap and turned her attention to Bishop Abram, who was slowly making his way to the podium at the front of the sanctuary. Her embarrassing Jonah? The thought nearly made her laugh out loud. Oh please...as if he didn't do an excellent job of that on his own. Katherine rolled her eyes heavenward when she caught him winking at a couple of single women sitting on the opposite side of the church.

"Really, Jonah, don't you have any manners?"

He chuckled at her remark before the Bishop garnered the congregation's attention. A hush fell over the crowd and they all bowed their heads when he started the service with a long prayer. She made a mental note to mend Jonah's shirt as soon as they returned home. Perhaps he didn't mind going out in public with tattered clothing, but it bothered her to no end. The last thing she wanted or needed was for the people in their little Amish village to think she was slacking in caring for her brother, a job she'd taken very seriously since their parents' death three years prior.

When Katherine opened her eyes, she was surprised to see someone had joined Bishop Abram behind the podium, but it was no ordinary person, and the stranger certainly wasn't from their community. The gentleman standing beside the Bishop was dressed in English clothing, sporting a short beard and mustache, and he held a cell phone in his right hand. Katherine felt her cheeks flush, and she tried not to stare, but he was quite handsome.

The congregation shared curious glances as the Bishop gestured to the man and introduced him as Dr. Steven Read, a newcomer to Lancaster, but no foreigner to the Amish. He explained how the doctor was raised in the faith as a child in western Pennsylvania, and that he'd discovered his calling in life during his Rumspringa when he was just sixteen years old. He'd practiced medicine ever since and had recently taken over Lancaster's small medical clinic after the previous owner retired from the field.

"My brothers and sisters, I hope you will join me in welcoming Dr. Read to Lancaster and to our community. Several of you have mentioned to me how time-consuming it is to make the trip to the clinic, and Dr. Read has generously volunteered to make house calls."

The excitement in the room was almost palpable and Katherine felt her stomach flutter with excitement also. She'd lost count of the numerous times she'd wrangled Jonah into their carriage and made the long drive to the clinic - sometimes in the dead of night and even during torrential downpours. As far as she knew, the previous doctor never made house calls, at least not to the Amish households, so this was a welcomed change for sure.

After the Bishop introduced Dr. Read and concluded his discussion over the services he would provide, Katherine expected the doctor to leave, but he didn't. Instead, he sat down on one of the front pews and joined in the service. A couple of hours later, when Bishop Abram asked if he'd like to close the service with a prayer, he didn't falter or try to beg his way out of it. He wholeheartedly accepted, and his prayer even received a rousing "amen" from the Bishop when he finished.

Katherine struggled in vain to keep from ogling him, but she couldn't help herself. There was something oddly fascinating about the man - and it wasn't just his rugged good looks either.

"Really, Katherine, don't you have any manners? Stop staring." Jonah mimicked as they stood to leave. Her cheeks burned a bright shade of red as she playfully elbowed him in the stomach, which made him laugh. Two of his close friends caught his attention as they waved to him from across the crowded room, and when he left her side to join them, she was grateful for the reprieve.

Bishop Abram and the doctor stood by the front door, and as Katherine watched him smile and introduce himself to each member of the congregation, she stole a glance toward the back door of the church. Unfortunately, the throng of people was too big to push through so a hasty retreat in the opposite direction wasn't possible.

"Dr. Read, this is Katherine Mills. She and her younger brother, Jonah, own and operate the local dairy farm."

Katherine jerked her head around, not realizing the fast-moving crowd had already nudged her to the front of the line. When she nearly bumped into the doctor, she took a couple of hesitant steps backward to regain her footing.

"H-hello. It's nice meeting you. Welcome to Lancaster," she stammered.

The doctor grinned and thanked her, and Katherine felt her heartrate escalate when the masculine aroma of his cologne wafted past her nose and left her temporarily dazed. He pulled a business card from his jacket pocket and handed it to her, and when their fingers touched, she held her breath.

"Please don't hesitate to call me anytime you have an emergency - day or night," he remarked.

She didn't trust herself to say anything else without sounding like an enamored schoolgirl, so she simply nodded before turning to leave. Perhaps it was just wishful thinking, but she could almost feel the doctors gaze on her as she walked away, which made her legs wobbly and sent a chill up her spine.

Katherine sighed.

She couldn't deny it. The new doctor in town had her spellbound.

* * * *

Steven squinted as he peered out his car window, trying to discern which of the small houses belonged to Miss Hannah Bowen. He glanced at his notepad again and mumbled the information he'd hastily scribbled down while rushing out the door of his clinic.

"House #142. Okay...where are you?"

It was his first medical call to the small Amish village since Bishop Abram introduced him to everyone the previous Sunday, and his stomach flip-flopped with equal parts excitement and fear. He wanted to make a good impression, but as he circled back for what felt like the hundredth time, he started to wonder if he may have bitten off more than he could chew. With the sun setting on the horizon, most of the houses looked identical in the fading light, from their brown tin roofs straight down to the white wooden swings on their front porches.

He strongly considered throwing in the towel until he caught sight of an older woman standing on some porch steps, waving her arms high in the air to get his attention. As he brought his car to a stop in front of the house, he caught sight of the small metallic numbers nailed to one of the porch columns - #142. When he turned off the ignition and stepped out with his medical bag in tow, the woman left the steps and walked around the vehicle to greet him.

"Miss Bowen?" he inquired.

She nodded and motioned toward the front door. "*Yah*, thank you so much for coming, Dr. Read. My son, William, woke up this morning with a fever, and he's been sleeping off and on all day, which isn't like him because he's usually full of energy."

He could tell by the way her voice shook that she was worried, and as they made their way inside the small wood framed house he understood why. A young man who couldn't have been more than twelve years old stood just inside the doorway, holding on to the back of a tall chair. His unruly brown hair was plastered to his skin and his face was a deathly shade of white.

"William!" Miss Bowen exclaimed. "What are you doing up?"

He opened his mouth but no words came out, which alarmed Steven right away. He noticed how William swayed precariously on his feet, and he rushed over to keep him upright before he toppled to the floor.

"Your mom is right. We should get you back to bed."

When he put his arm around William's waist to keep him steady, his heart plummeted to his feet when he felt the intense heat emanating from William's body through his clothing.

"Miss Bowen, can you please bring me some ice wrapped in a bath cloth or dish towel? He's burning up with fever and we need to get it down as quickly as we can."

Tears cascaded down her face as she directed him to William's room before racing to the kitchen. Once William was lying comfortably on his bed, Steven opened his medical bag and removed a stethoscope and otoscope so he could listen to his chest and examine his ears and throat. Fortunately, his lungs sounded clear, but his ears and throat were extremely red and inflamed, which could explain the fever.

Miss Bowen returned with the ice and placed the towel against William's forehead. He opened his eyelids slightly and moaned, and Miss Bowen kissed his cheeks and caressed them gently with her fingers.

"It's okay, sweetheart. I know you're hurting, but Dr. Read is going to help you feel better. I promise."

He appreciated her show of confidence in him, especially since he was basically a stranger to her small town, and he smiled before continuing his examination. The lymph nodes in William's neck were swollen and tender, and although the ice brought his fever down somewhat, it still wasn't where Steven felt it needed to be.

"Miss Bowen, William's ears and throat are badly infected, and I would like to give him a shot of Rocephin, if it's alright with you. This medicine will take care of his fever more quickly than taking oral medication, and I'm worried if we don't get his fever down soon he might have a seizure."

As soon as Steven mentioned giving him a shot, William's eyelids flew open and he fervently shook his head while Miss Bowen struggled to keep him still. "No, no, no...I don't want a shot..." he mumbled.

Steven reached out and touched her hand. "Miss Bowen, I know how you feel about traditional medicine, and I understand because I was raised in an Amish household, but I promise I wouldn't recommend this if I didn't feel it was absolutely necessary."

The tears kept rolling down her cheeks, and the inner battle going on inside was more than evident by the pained look on her face. He felt guilty for suggesting something he knew was against her faith, but he had to do what he felt was right for William. Whether she decided to do it or not was totally up to her, but he feared there would be dire consequences if she refused. William's eyes swelled with tears, which only added to his misery, and he swallowed hard to try and keep it together. He dearly loved his job, but there were moments when he wished he'd never left home, and this was one of those times.

"Luke! Come here please!" Miss Bowen called.

Steven heard a door open in the hallway moments before a youngster appeared in the doorway. This child looked younger than

William by a couple of years, but they were almost identical with their wavy brown hair and blue eyes.

"What's wrong with brother?" he asked. His eyes were wide and expressive as he gazed at William, and Steven felt helpless and unsure of what to say. He'd tended to many children in his line of work, but having none of his own left him at a disadvantage sometimes.

"He's sick, and I need you to get Mr. Jonah right away. Do you understand?"

Without another word, Luke turned and bolted down the hallway and out the front door.

"Jonah Mills has been like a second father to my boys since my husband passed away last year," she explained. "Maybe he can help keep William calm while you give him the shot."

Steven thought for a moment. *Jonah Mills.* The name sounded vaguely familiar, and his spirits lifted when he remembered Bishop Abram introducing Jonah as Katherine's younger brother. He'd met dozens of people that Sunday in church, but Katherine was the only person he hadn't been able to stop thinking about, especially after Bishop Abram made it a point to mention to him that she wasn't married.

A few minutes later, Steven heard the front door open and he held his breath anxiously as heavy footsteps echoed down the hallway before Luke reappeared with Jonah by his side. They were both out of breath and Jonah's face paled when he saw William lying motionless on the bed. Steven leaned over and looked behind them, hoping that Katherine may have followed, but his hopes vanished when he realized it was just the two of them.

Jonah knelt by the bed and William's eyelids fluttered open when he heard him speak. "Hey, buddy. I got here as fast as I could."

Miss Bowen reciprocated the dishcloth between different spots on William's body, from his forehead to his cheeks and downward to his chest. "Dr. Read was just telling us how it would make William feel better if he gave him a shot to bring down his fever, but he doesn't like that idea very much."

Jonah nodded as if he understood before grabbing William's right hand and giving it a squeeze. "Our baseball game won't be the same next weekend if we don't have our best hitter there to help lead us to victory. I bet Dr. Read is great at giving shots. You probably won't even feel it."

He gave Steven a stern look, as if needing reassurance, so Steven reiterated to William that he would do his very best to make the shot as pain-free as possible. A couple of tears escaped and rolled down William's cheeks, but he ultimately agreed to it, and while Jonah, Luke, and Miss Bowen showered him with words of encouragement, Steven removed the bottle of Rocephin and a syringe from his medical bag and prepared the dosage.

Although it seemed to last an eternity, the amount of time it took between turning William over on his left side and Steven giving him the shot in his hip was mere seconds, and he was pleasantly surprised when William smiled at him when it was over.

"See? That wasn't so bad," Jonah said. "I'm really proud of you, buddy. You'll start feeling better in no time."

After Steven returned his supplies to his bag, he gestured for Miss Bowen to follow him into the hallway. While Luke took over holding the dishcloth to William's forehead, Jonah regaled him with jokes that had him laughing and smiling. When Steven saw the color return to William's cheeks, he breathed a huge sigh of relief.

"I'll come by tomorrow afternoon and check on him," Steven whispered, so they wouldn't be overheard. "Hopefully he'll be feeling a lot better and he won't have to take antibiotics, but we'll just play it by ear and see how he's doing."

Before Miss Bowen could reply, there was a knock on the front door, and Steven's heart skipped a beat when she opened it and he saw Katherine standing on the other side. Her long brown hair was pulled back and tied with a white ribbon at the base of her neck, and her cheeks were flushed a bright shade of pink.

"Is something wrong?" she asked, while trying to catch her breath. "I would have been here sooner, but I was getting dinner out of the oven when Luke came by, and all I heard was "William needs you" before he and Jonah took off running. I had no idea what was going on and I ran the whole way and..."

Miss Bowen raised a hand to stop her from staying anything else, which was probably a good thing, because she appeared on the verge of hyperventilating. When Miss Bowen ushered her inside and she caught sight of Steven standing in the living room, she flashed him a bashful smile. "Hello, Dr. Read. How are you?"

Steven felt tongue-tied at first, but he forced himself to say something – *anything*. "I'm doing good. Please...call me Steven."

Miss Bowen excused herself and returned to William's room, and suddenly the room became eerily quiet and very awkward. Katherine crossed her arms over her chest and rocked back and forth on her heels while Steven stuffed his hands inside his pants pockets and tried to come up with some topic of conversation.

Why was it so difficult talking to her? It wasn't as if he hadn't talked to other women before. It was ridiculous, really, and he felt embarrassed over his lack of wisdom when it came to the opposite sex.

"How is William doing?" she asked.

Steven cleared his throat before trusting himself to say anything coherent without tripping over his own tongue. "His throat and ears are badly infected, but I believe he's going to be okay. At first, he was afraid of getting a shot, but Jonah was able to talk him into it."

His comment made her smile, and Steven's heart fluttered. She was so beautiful, and her happiness lit up the entire room. He couldn't help but wonder if she even realized just how beautiful she was.

"Jonah is a lot older than William, but they are really close."

Katherine walked over to a chair in the living room and sat down, so Steven followed suit and took a seat on the sofa across from her. He could hear the muffled whispers streaming in the hallway, and his spirits lifted when he heard laughter coming from William's bedroom.

"Miss Bowen said he's become somewhat of a father figure since her husband died," he replied.

Katherine sat upright in her seat and flattened her palms on top of her knees. She looked uncomfortable, and he hoped it wasn't his presence that bothered her. If anything, he felt more at peace talking to her than he had since his arrival in Lancaster two months prior.

"*Yah*, I think it's good for them both. Our parents passed away three years ago, and there's only so much a sister knows about hunting, fishing, and farming. I do my fair share of it, but he needs more male friends in his life to talk to and spend time with."

Steven couldn't help but envy their closeness. When he didn't return home following his Rumspringa, he ruined any possibility of seeing or talking to his parents and two older brothers ever again. He didn't regret his decision to follow his dream of becoming a doctor, but he couldn't deny there were times when he wished he could go back and do things differently just to hear their voices one more time.

The sound of footsteps on the hardwood floor interrupted their conversation a few seconds before Jonah and Miss Bowen entered the living room.

"William is sleeping," she announced. "Thank you for coming so quickly, Dr. Read. He already seems to be feeling much better."

Steven took that as his cue to leave, even though it was the last thing he wanted to do. He would've been content just to sit and talk to Katherine all night. When he stood to go, she did the same, nearly causing them to bump into each other. They were so close he could see the tiny line of freckles that danced across the bridge of her nose.

"I should be going," he said. "I need to stop by the diner before they close."

Jonah waved a hand in the air, as if dismissing his comment. "Isabelle's Diner in Lancaster? No way. You can come to our house for a proper dinner. Katherine made her famous meatloaf and mashed potatoes."

He looked at Katherine, and he could tell by the bewildered expression on her face that she was shocked by her brother's suggestion. Because of that, he thought it would be best to politely decline, but before he had the opportunity, Katherine was agreeing with him. "I think that's a great idea."

He couldn't tell if she truly meant it or not, but he didn't want to be rude and ruin any chance he might have of seeing her again.

"Umm...okay," he replied, hesitantly. "Miss Bowen, I'll see you tomorrow afternoon, but if you need me before then, please don't hesitate to call me again."

She nodded before wishing them a good evening and leading them to the door. As Steven crossed the porch with Jonah and Katherine, he couldn't help but wonder what other surprises the rest of the night would hold.

* * * *

The following afternoon, while Jonah was busy gathering milk in the barn, Katherine took her cup of coffee to the back porch so she could enjoy a few minutes of peace and quiet. She also needed the coffee to keep her awake, since she'd gotten little sleep the night before. Although dinner ended early, she and Steven talked until midnight, and the remaining hours until daybreak were spent tossing and turning when she was unable to get him off her mind.

Katherine sighed contentedly as she recalled how easy it was to talk to him and the way his laughter reverberated off the walls in her tiny kitchen and wrapped around her heart. But despite the good that warmed her soul, there was also the hard truth that he'd been shunned from his own community when he didn't return from his Rumspringa.

He was now an English man who lived by English customs, and that was something she couldn't easily ignore, no matter how wildly her heart raced whenever he was near.

"What is causing such deep concentration, sister?"

Startled from her daydream, Katherine jumped and nearly spilled her full cup of coffee as Jonah laughed and bounded up the back-porch steps. When he sat down in the rocking chair beside her, she gave him a sideways glance without trying to hide her annoyance.

"I bet you were thinking about the new doctor in town," he joked. "Am I right?"

She didn't reply, but the blush in her cheeks must have given her away, as Jonah slapped his hand on the arm of the rocker and howled with laughter. "I knew it!"

Katherine steadied her cup of coffee on her lap and looked out across the large field behind their house. Rain clouds hovered in the distance and cast a shadow over the yard, but she didn't mind the impending rain. In fact, she welcomed it. If anything, it matched her solemn mood.

"I guess you think you're pretty clever, the way you snuck past me and invited him to eat dinner with us last night."

Jonah laughed again. "Oh, come on. You know you enjoyed it. I could hear the two of you talking and laughing from my bedroom."

Katherine sighed once again. "You're forgetting the circumstances, Jonah. Even if I wanted to be with Steven, it wouldn't be possible. He's already been shunned from our way of life, so no one would accept him."

Jonah frowned. "I don't think that's true. I know he and Bishop Abram are good friends, so there might be more hope than you realize."

Katherine took a sip of her coffee and let the heat from it sink into her bones. There was a lot to consider, but she was honestly afraid to get her hopes up and risk them being trampled on. There were also more important things to keep in mind besides her own feelings over the matter.

"I'm not going to leave you, Jonah. I made a promise to myself when mom and dad died that I would watch over you and take care of you – always."

From the corner of her eye, she caught Jonah turning in the rocker so he could face her, but she refused to look at him. She knew what would be behind those brown eyes, and she didn't want to see it. She'd lost count of the times they'd discussed their future and she didn't want to hear him proclaim again how he would be fine on his own someday. Perhaps he would when he found the right woman to settle down with, but until then he was her responsibility.

"Katherine, I love you, but you have *got* to accept the fact that I'm eighteen years old and a grown man."

Katherine cocked a weary eyebrow as she glanced in his direction. "I'm fully aware of that, Jonah."

He took off his hat and propped it on top of his knee. "There's no way I could ever properly thank you for everything you've done for me, but I want you to be happy. That's all I've ever wanted."

Katherine took another sip of her coffee. "But I am happy."

Jonah reached out and laid a hand on her arm, causing her to stop rocking and look his way. He had the sincerest expression on his face – something she wasn't used to seeing, since he spent most of his time cracking jokes and doing his best to make her laugh.

"I'm talking about the happiness I saw last night, Katherine. I didn't miss the way your eyes lit up when Steven was here, and I don't want you to risk losing that over me. Father taught me everything I need to know about running his business, and I can take care of myself and this farm."

Katherine let her eyes sweep over the property before she shook her head. "There's no way you can handle this all on your own."

Jonah's lips curled upward into a sly grin. "Who said I would be alone? I do plan on getting married someday, and I even have my heart set on someone special right now. I have for quite a while now."

Katherine sat up straight in her seat, nearly spilling her coffee again. "Really? Who is she?"

Jonah rested his head against the back of the rocking chair and grinned. "Don't even try and change the subject. We're talking about *you* – not me. You'll find out soon enough."

Katherine couldn't help but wonder who he was referring to, as she carefully considered every single woman in their community. There were several who came to mind, but she knew he wouldn't divulge his secret no matter how hard she pushed, so she decided to let it pass – at least for the time being.

"So, what do you think I should do?" she asked. "Should I talk to Bishop Abram first to see where he stands with us seeing each other?"

Jonah looked up at the tin roof and shook his head. "I think you should follow your heart. What do you *want* to do first?"

Katherine smiled. That was an easy question. "I want to talk to Steven and see if he feels the same way about me."

Jonah grabbed his hat and jumped to his feet. "That's what I was hoping you'd say. You should do that...*now*."

Katherine nearly choked on her coffee. "What? I didn't mean right this second."

Unfortunately, he wouldn't be swayed. Jonah took the coffee cup from her hand and disappeared inside the house. When he returned a couple of minutes later, the cup was nowhere to be seen and he had an umbrella hooked over his forearm.

"Take this in case it starts raining on your way to the phone."

He pulled Steven's business card from his shirt pocket and handed it to her, along with the umbrella. Katherine looked toward the dark clouds in the west and frowned. What if she didn't make it back before it started pouring rain? The phone shanty was a mile or so from their home, and the storm clouds were approaching fast.

Katherine stood up straight and squared her shoulders. No, it was now or never. If she kept waiting she would lose her nerve...and she would never hear the end of it from Jonah. Katherine opened the back door and grabbed her rubber boots, which were nestled in a corner just inside the doorway, and slipped them on before she changed her mind.

"Wish me luck!" she called to her brother, as she bounded off the back-porch steps and walked hurriedly toward the main dirt road. Her heart pounded furiously inside her chest, but it was a wonderful feeling – a mixture of excitement, anxiousness, and hope all rolled into one.

She prayed out loud as she walked, which bolstered her confidence. She refused to believe that God would bring Steven into her life only to break her heart by keeping them apart. With any luck, Bishop Abram and the others would be on their side as well.

* * * *

Steven unlocked his front door and retreated inside his house. He'd managed to get his groceries from the store to the car before the rain started, but now he had to carry them from the car to his house before the paper bags turned to mush and his groceries spilled all over the driveway. He groaned as the fumbled for the light switch. He didn't even own an umbrella.

Steven pulled his cell phone from his jacket pocket and plugged it into his charger on the kitchen counter. He'd noticed the voicemail icon blinking while driving home, but there wasn't enough battery life remaining to check it. He did see on the caller ID that it was the number to the Amish village, which was strange. He'd visited William Bowen around noon, and he was doing much better, so it couldn't be his mother calling.

At least, he hoped it wasn't. Steven's heart sank when he considered the possibility William may have relapsed. He quickly got the groceries inside as he waited for the battery to charge, and when he finished putting the items away, he saw a green light blinking on his phone, signaling that the battery was charged enough for him to check his messages. When he heard the voice on the other end of the line, he was taken by surprise.

"Hello, Steven. I...I've never left a message before, so I don't know if I'm doing this right or not. First off, I'm okay and there isn't an emergency. I apologize if I'm being too forward by calling you, but...I just wanted to let you know how much I enjoyed our conversation last night..."

His heart skipped a beat. *Katherine.* There was a long pause, but he could hear a loud noise in the background that sounded like thunder, and Steven frowned when he pictured her in the village's small phone shanty while the rain poured outside.

"I know our lives are very different, but...that hasn't stopped me from thinking about you. I really don't know what else to say other than I hope to see you again...soon."

Click.

Steven glanced at his wristwatch as he gathered up his cell phone and car keys. Going by the timestamp on his caller ID, fifteen minutes had passed since Katherine's call. As he raced to his vehicle, he silently prayed that the emotion he heard in her voice was the same as he'd felt since the day he met her. She was right about their paths in life being completely different, but he hoped that wouldn't stand in the way of something he felt in his heart could be very special. He'd grown up with the same Amish values and traditions, so there was no denying it could possibly be an uphill battle.

Steven roared the car to life and took off toward Katherine's house. The rain had died down to a drizzle, but the dirt road leading to the village was slippery and sent his wheels spinning. He took his foot off the accelerator and tapped his fingers impatiently against the steering wheel. He wanted to get to her as quickly as he could, but he also needed to get there in one piece.

As he neared Katherine's driveway, he caught sight of her walking across the front yard to her house. When his headlights shined upon her, he noticed how the small umbrella she carried did nothing more than protect her face from the rain. The rest of her was soaking wet.

Steven parked the car and took off on foot to meet her. She stopped when she saw him coming, and when he put his arm around her waist and led her toward the front porch, she didn't object. Just as he guessed, she was soaked to the skin and she shivered so much her teeth chattered. He opened the door and ushered her inside, and while Jonah went to the kitchen to get her something warm to drink, Steven grabbed a blanket from the sofa and draped it around her shoulders.

"What in the world were you thinking, Katherine?" he murmured. "You're going to catch your death of cold..."

She stopped him mid-sentence by placing a hand against his chest. "If you got my message then it was worth it."

Steven ran his fingers through her wet hair and moved it away from her neck, letting his fingertips glide softly against her neck. "I did."

Jonah returned with a steaming cup of coffee, but the moment he saw them huddled close together, he placed the cup on a table beside the sofa and excused himself from the room – but not before winking and grinning at them both.

Steven pulled the blanket tighter around Katherine's shoulders. "You should change clothes before you get sick...doctor's orders."

She laughed softly and the beautiful sound melted his heart and weakened his knees. When she took his hand, and led him toward the sofa, he followed like a love-struck teenager. Once they were seated, he picked up the coffee mug and encouraged her take a couple of sips. The color returned to her cheeks, although a bit slowly for his liking, and his first concern was getting some heat coursing through her veins.

"Steven...am I crazy for thinking this could turn into something more than just friendship?" she asked.

He squeezed her hands and moved closer. "No, I don't think that's crazy at all. I know we haven't known each other long, but I feel the same way. Do you remember me telling you last night how I wished I could go back and do things differently – how I never would have left my family?"

She nodded.

"I feel very strongly about that, and I know the odds may be stacked against me, but I really feel like Bishop Abram and the community will give me the opportunity to return to the fold when they see how I feel about you. All we do is pray over it and hope for the best."

When Katherine leaned into him and gently kissed his lips, he was caught off guard, but happily so. The moment may have been brief, but it left his heart racing wildly in his chest.

"We'll get through this together," she replied, emphatically.

Steven nodded – more certain in his conviction than ever before. He knew deep in his heart they were meant to be together...and he was ready and willing to do whatever it took to make that dream a reality.

Amish Decisions

Samantha Collier

Rachel looked out the window, watching the fierce blizzard swirl around the farmhouse. It had been building for days.

Last night, it had intensified so much that her sleep was disturbed. The old house creaked and moaned as the wind picked up. She had risen to her bedroom window, amazed at the snowflakes swirling as if in a vortex. The cold had punctured her skin like a million needles.

This morning, it was worse. She watched, anxiously, as her father battled alone through it, securing the animals as best as he could.

Two day until Christmas. The world was white, and frightening. Somehow, nature reflected her inner turmoil. She had not been herself, these past weeks.

Sighing, Rachel wrapped her shawl tighter around her shoulders. The temperature had dropped, again. The fire roaring in the corner seemed to throw out little warmth. At least they had enough firewood to outlast the storm. How long could the blizzard last? Would Christmas still go ahead?

Suddenly, she heard her father shouting outside. What was wrong? She craned her neck to see, but the swirl of white was so intense outside that it was impossible.

The front door opened, sending in a blast of snow. It was her father, of course. But as Rachel turned, she was shocked to see two figures with him. Both tall. One was dressed in black, in the typical Amish fashion. The other wore jeans and a huge snow coat, in the English style. Two men, covered in snow, stomping their boots onto the mat.

Her father struggled to shut the door against the wind. Then the trio walked into the living room.

Rachel gasped. How could this be? For she knew the two men. They were as different from each other as chalk and cheese. As far as she knew, they didn't know each other. How was it that they were together, in her living room?

And worse, stuck together in her living room. For this blizzard was here to stay, at least for today. There was little indication that it would abate. The two men were marooned with her family at their farmhouse. The neighbours were miles away in either direction. And the roads would be blocked.

It was as if they had planned it, but how could they have?

Two men. Both known to Rachel. Had God planned it? He knew the decision that she had to make. Had he put both here to make her decide?

***

The Amish man was Abraham. She had known him forever.

She remembered the first time that she had seen him. They had been children, going to school together. Someone had pulled her *kapps* from behind as she sat at her desk, making her cry. Well, she had only been five years old. But the boy that she had been told to sit next to reached over and gave her his handkerchief. Through her sobs, she had turned and looked at him.

"Are you alright?" he whispered, looking at her in concern.

She nodded, slowly. Her sobs abated.

"I'm Abraham," he said. "Don't worry, I'll look out for you."

And he had. Abraham had been like the brother she had never had. In the playground, he would watch her, making sure she was okay. They rarely played together, but she knew he was always there. Like a guardian angel.

They had grown up, as children must. She was always conscious of him in her life. His eyes would shine when he looked at her. A constant, like the moon and the stars in the night sky.

Rachel could pinpoint the moment when it had all changed between them.

Rummspringa had happened. Rachel had been curious about the world, and travelled to stay with English friends in the city. She had seen so many wonderful things; the English world intoxicated her.

Should she stay in her community, safe and loved, or should she spread her wings wider? What did God intend for her life?

She had met him in town, when she had returned. Literally ran into him as she crossed the road to do her shopping.

"Abraham!" She had been joyful, to see him again. But he hadn't smiled back.

"Rachel." He inclined his head, quietly assessing her. "I haven't seen you for a while. Where have you been?"

"Oh, Abraham," she gushed. Her eyes shone in excitement. "I have been to the city! It was wonderful. So many things to see and do."

He had frowned, slightly. "*Jah,* it can be exciting," he had replied. He looked her over. "You've changed, Rachel."

"Have I?" She twirled around, inviting his admiration. But it wasn't forthcoming. His statement hadn't been a compliment. She felt her excitement puncture slowly. Why was he so disapproving?

"Well, it was nice to see you," she replied. She didn't smile at him. "I must go, now. Mamm is waiting for me."

He had bowed again, and walked away without a backward glance.

And that was it. She hadn't talked to him much since. A distance that could not be bridged had sprung up between them. She heard that he was courting Eva, a girl they had both gone to school with. She had been sad that they hadn't remained friends, but philosophical, too. For her world had changed entirely.

David, the English man in her living room, had happened.

She had met him on *rummspringa.* He was a friend of the family she had stayed with. She had been shy with him, at first. She hadn't met many English men. But he had been gentle and sweet with her, asking how she was enjoying the city. Then he had invited her to see the latest exhibition of an artist that was showing at a gallery.

She had hesitated, just for a moment. But then she had accepted.

He picked her up in his car, whirling through the city streets. She wasn't used to cars, and felt quite giddy.

They had walked through the gallery together, admiring the paintings. She didn't know much about art, but David was well informed. He pointed out how the artist had used texture and shading to build the paintings. He knew a lot about the history of art, and the influences in the paintings.

She hadn't said much. It was like she was a sponge, soaking in all the knowledge that was being heaped upon her. It was fascinating, and alluring.

Could she become a part of this world?

But then, *rummspringa* had ended, and she had returned home. Her afternoon at the gallery with David acquired the aura of a pleasant dream. She knew it had happened, and that it had been wonderful. But she had not seen him again.

Until he had unexpectedly visited her.

Mamm had been shocked when she opened the door on the tall English man that day.

"*Jah*?" she had inquired, looking him up and down. "Can I help you?"

David had smiled. "Yes, I was wondering if Rachel was here," he said.

Rachel had heard his voice and come to the door, amazed. "It's alright, Mamm," she said. "This is David, a friend of the Baileys. I met him on my stay there."

Mamm had raised her eyebrows, but let him enter.

David had walked into the house, a bit awkwardly. She had made them coffee; her mother had left them to talk alone in the parlour. Rachel was mystified. Why was he here?

It turned out that David had friends in the area, and knew she was close by.

"I was wondering," he said, looking at her carefully, "whether you would like to see the gallery in the nearest town. And then maybe, get a coffee?"

Rachel had considered. She was very fond of David, but he was an Englisher. Would going on outings with him encourage him to think that she might court him?

She didn't even know, herself. It was like she was being pulled in two directions. One path, very clear and obvious – getting baptised into her community, and living the life her family wanted her to. The other path was thorny, and wound into complicated areas – to not be baptised, and so become a part of the English world. Her father had started pressuring her recently about it, to make the choice. He also wanted her to consider marriage.

I'm only nineteen, Rachel thought to herself, a bit desperately. Why must I make a choice?

But she did. If only she could be like her best friend, Lovina, who was very sure and comfortable about staying within the community. But then, Lovina had courted several local Amish boys, and knew how to talk to them. Lovina wasn't shy and nervy, like Rachel.

Rachel took a sip of her coffee, thinking deeply. David needed an answer. He had sought her out, and besides, it would be impolite to refuse him. And she did like him, very much.

"I would love to," she replied. David smiled.

She very much felt like she was on the edge of a precipice, where one wrong step could see her careering into an abyss.

***

Rachel looked at the two men, frozen from the blizzard. She could feel her mouth open, like a gaping fish. Surprise had rendered her speechless.

Abraham spoke first. "You look surprised, Rachel," he said. "I was travelling along the road when I saw a car broken down."

"Yes," David continued, looking at Abraham, "my car suddenly broke down. The electrics I think; the lights were dimming and the radio flickering on and off. Luckily, Abraham happened by and gave me a lift in his buggy."

"But the blizzard caught us, and your farmhouse was closest," Abraham continued. "So here we are."

Both men looked at her, expectantly.

Rachel roused herself. "Please, sit down," she said. At least her powers of speech had returned. "I will make a pot of coffee, and inform my mother. She is sewing in her room."

Abraham and David sat down, looking at each other warily. You could cut the air with a knife, Rachel thought darkly.

They would all just have to make the best of it. At least until the blizzard cleared.

***

As Rachel made the coffee, she thought back to the week before, when she had gone into town with David to the gallery.

It had started out perfectly fine. They had perused the gallery, and Rachel had enjoyed it again. She was getting a stronger sense of art in the English world; was becoming infected with David's passion for it. Once again, the world seemed to shift and slide for her. She could – if she made the choice – do this all the time.

But what of her family? They would be devastated if she decided not to be baptised. Oh, it wasn't the same as if she left them after being baptised, she knew that. She wouldn't be shunned. But she would still be forever separate from them. She would be able to see them, but she knew it would never be the same.

Yet, the siren's call of the gallery beckoned her. A life, perhaps, with this man? Where they could talk about art, view it, travel together?

She was getting ahead of herself, of course. She didn't know how she felt about David.

It seemed she didn't know anything, anymore. The confusion, the push and pull of it, was like a fog within her brain.

They had a coffee afterwards, where David had spoken enthusiastically about the exhibition, and the artist.

"Would you like to come with me to another?" he asked, his eyes shining. "There is one in the next town starting next week."

"Maybe," Rachel had replied, frowning. "I'm not sure."

"Didn't you enjoy today?" he asked quickly. He seemed to really want to hear the answer.

"*Jah*, it was wonderful," she said. She paused, trying to gather her thoughts. "It's just that I am confused. I don't know if it is the best idea, doing this too much. It lures me away from my community."

He nodded, seeming to understand. "But then you can make an informed decision, can't you?" he pressed. "The more knowledge you have, the more power."

"Maybe," she replied, sipping her coffee. "Or maybe it is more temptation." She smiled, then shook her head. "I will let you know, David."

The shop bell rang, and someone walked through the door. She turned to look.

It was Abraham.

Would he acknowledge her? He barely spoke to her, anymore. It was sad; she remembered when they had been friends. Must everything change?

He had seen her. He paused, as if considering if he should approach.

Her heart lifted when he turned in her direction, heading toward the table.

"Rachel." He nodded at them both, his eyes widening slightly as he assessed David. Was he terribly shocked to see her here, having coffee with an Englisher? Would he disapprove?

"Abraham," she said, smiling widely. "It is so good to see you! This is my friend, David."

The men shook hands. Rachel could see David was quietly assessing Abraham, as well.

"So," Abraham said. He shifted awkwardly. "Have you been busy?"

"We've just been to see the latest exhibition at the gallery," Rachel replied. "Oh, you would love it, Abraham! Such beautiful paintings."

Abraham nodded, slowly. "I am glad you enjoyed it," he said. "Well, I must be off." He tilted his hat, at them both. Then he turned to the counter, to order what he had come in for.

"An old friend of yours?" asked David.

"One of my oldest," answered Rachel, a little sadly. "But we have drifted apart, lately. He doesn't want to be friends with me anymore, it seems." She looked down at her coffee, biting her lip.

"Well, he doesn't deserve you, then," said David, reaching out to put his hand over hers.

She stared down at his hand, covering her own. Was it seemly, especially in public? But she didn't move it.

And it was at that moment that Abraham turned back to them.

He frowned, looking at their hands. She could feel tension zip through his body, making him stand straighter. Almost as if he were about to pounce.

She quickly removed her hand, blushing. What must Abraham think of her?

The moment seemed to stretch on, forever. David locked eyes with Abraham, who stared him down. Tension filled the air.

Eventually, Abraham had broken it. He had simply turned and walked out of the shop, not looking back.

Rachel's eyes filled with tears. She couldn't bear him thinking badly of her. But what could she do now?

***

And now they were both sitting in her parlour, awaiting coffee. Life was strange, Rachel reflected as she picked up the cups and took them into the waiting men.

Her father had re-joined them, and was in the process of throwing a log onto the fire. It hissed and crackled as it fell, shooting out sparks up into the chimney. Inside, all was warm and bright; outside, the world had turned to white, a swirling vortex of snowflakes. The old house creaked and groaned under the pressure.

Rachel looked at the candles adorning the windows. The Christmas baskets, that had been prepared for the elderly in the community by her mother, were sitting on the floor, awaiting delivery. Would they be able to deliver them, now? It was only two days until Christmas. Rachel's heart constricted at the thought that those baskets would not get to their recipients in time.

Abraham was still sitting, staring at the fire and chatting with her father. David had stood up, and was looking out the window. He was frowning.

"It doesn't look like I'll be making it home for Christmas," he said, a little sadly. Rachel walked up to him, smiling.

"It might clear," she said, staring out. "I have seen blizzards suddenly blow themselves out. You might still make it." She pondered the thought of spending Christmas away from her family. She simply couldn't imagine it. She pictured them all gathered, eating a huge roast chicken with gravy and all the trimmings, just like they always did. Afterwards, there would be pie.

Christmas was about family. She shuddered. If she decided not to get baptised, she would no longer be a part of it. She couldn't bear the thought.

She could feel Abraham's eyes on her. Was he disapproving of her, again? Why had he suddenly decided that he didn't like her anymore? It was so perplexing. To have been so close to him, for so long.

They made stilted conversation as the day wore into the night. Her mother made up the spare bedrooms, and eventually they had all retired for the night. Rachel breathed a sigh of relief; she was glad to have escaped.

In bed, she pondered further. Eventually she turned to her bible, seeking comfort. A verse from Proverbs leapt out at her: "Trust in the Lord with all your heart, and do not lean on your own understanding. In all your ways acknowledge him, and he will make straight your paths."

She reflected. Perhaps there was her answer. She had been trying so hard to solve the dilemma, on an intellectual level. Perhaps she needed to stop thinking, and start trusting God. If she calmed her mind enough, he would lead her where she was supposed to go. She needed to stop fighting so hard.

She sighed, frowning. In the confusion of the two men staying unexpectedly, she had forgotten to get herself a glass of water before bed, as was her habit. She got up, sliding on her slippers and dressing gown, padding quietly down the stairs.

She had just turned on the tap and was filling the glass when she heard a sound behind her. She turned. David was standing there, looking at her.

Rachel instinctively tightened the belt on her dressing gown. This wasn't good; she was in her night attire, and didn't have her prayer *kapps* on. He shouldn't see her like this. She took the glass, smiling slightly at him as she walked past him.

He grabbed her arm, making her turn around to face him.

"David," she said, under her breath. "What are you doing? You are hurting me."

In response, he gripped her arm tighter, pulling her against him. The glass wobbled precariously in her hand. She didn't like the way that he was looking at her, not at all. What had suddenly come over him?

"Rachel, I want to kiss you," he said. Her eyes widened, in horror.

"No," she whispered. "It's not proper. This is my home, and you must respect our rules. I don't know how I feel about you, David. I know I like you as a friend."

He let go of her arm, suddenly, so that she stumbled backwards. Water spilt from the glass, slopping onto the floor.

"I should have known," he hissed at her. "You've been leading me on, all this time. Don't act innocent."

"I have not!" she replied. The accusation stung her. "You wanted to spend time with me, as a friend. That's what we've been doing. I never led you to believe anything else!"

He looked at her, witheringly. Then he turned and walked out of the room.

She leaned against the kitchen bench, breathing heavily.

What had just happened? She couldn't believe it. This was David, who had been nothing but kind and tender with her. Where had this sudden anger toward her come from? What had she done wrong?

Her eyes filled with tears of confusion and hurt. She had wanted to be part of the English world, had been dipping her toes into it. It had seemed expansive, full of things she wanted to explore. But this...this was a side of it, that she didn't like at all.

Was there truth in David's accusations? She had no idea. She was used to her community, where things progressed slowly and in sequence. Perhaps things were done differently in the English world. How would she know, after all?

Shaking slightly, she slowly walked back upstairs to her bedroom, climbing into bed. She had asked God for an answer, to lead her to decide. Perhaps, he had done just that.

But the fact remained: how on earth was she going to face David, in the morning?

***

Rachel stared out the window the next morning, breathing a sigh of relief. The blizzard was over. They were no longer stuck in the house.

She walked outside, grabbing her basket as she went. She needed to collect the eggs. Half of her hoped that David would be gone by the time she got inside. She didn't think that she could look him in the face, again.

Contradictory thoughts raced through her head, chasing each other. On the one hand, she felt anger toward him. How could he have done what he did? But on the other hand, she felt like she must have done something to provoke it. Something that she had no awareness of.

Her eyes filled with tears, again. It was better that she remain out here, amongst the hens. She didn't think that she could trust herself around anyone. She might burst into tears at the slightest thing.

The girls had not laid very many, of course. They never produced much, in winter. She could have completed the chore quickly, but she lagged.

She heard a noise, behind her. Her heart was gripped with fear. It wasn't David, was it?

But no. It was Abraham, walking up to her. "*Gutentag*," he called.

"*Gutentag*," she called back. She could feel her voice shake. She needed to get herself together.

"You are taking your time," he said, frowning as he looked in her basket. "Not many, today." He paused, looking at her. "I just wanted you to know, your friend David has left. He said he was in a hurry, and couldn't say good bye to you." Abraham frowned. "He was acting strangely, or stranger than he usually acts, at any rate."

Rachel's eyes glimmered with tears. She bit her lip. Don't say anything, she told herself fiercely.

"Rachel," Abraham said, softly. "What is wrong?"

She sat down, abruptly. Abraham sat down beside her.

"It's nothing," she said, wiping her eyes with the back of her hand. "I'm just being silly. I slept badly last night."

He said nothing, just let her catch her breath. But his eyes narrowed.

"Rachel," he said. "Look at me."

She turned her face, reluctantly, toward him.

"What did he do to you?" he whispered. "I'll go after him, this minute."

"No!" She reached out, laying a hand on his arm. He looked down at it.

"Then tell me what is wrong," he said.

"It's just a misunderstanding," she said. "David thought...that there was an expectation in our friendship. I had to tell him there wasn't. He wasn't happy – that is why he left this morning, so abruptly. He obviously didn't want to speak to me."

"What happened? Did he hurt you?" His face was dark.

She laughed, a little tremulously. "Oh, no," she whispered. "Not physically, anyway. He hurt my feelings, but that's okay. I should have known better."

"What are you talking about?" He said, frowning. "Known better than what? Rachel, the only thing that you should have known was to stay away from that man. I know you think that I don't like him just because he's English, but it's not that. I could tell what kind of man he was, straight away. He was trying to take advantage of you."

Rachel hung her head. The tears that had been threatening spilled over.

"Don't cry, Rachel," he said, gently. "I can't bear it, to see you like this."

"What can't you bear?" she cried, suddenly. "Why do you even care? You haven't been my friend in a long time, Abraham. Why should you suddenly decide what is good for me, and what isn't? Friends don't treat each other like this. Friends are there for each other, through thick and thin."

Abraham's hands balled into fists. "I couldn't watch it," he said, slowly. "I couldn't watch what you were doing. Toying with the English world. I thought you were going, Rachel. I thought you were making the decision to leave our community, and it made me so sad."

He took a deep breath. "And then, when I saw you hanging around with *him*." He spat the word, as if it was something distasteful. "I knew straight away what kind of a man he was. But you had stars in her eyes, talking about art and life away from here."

Rachel got to her feet, grabbing the basket. "Well, isn't that nice," she said. "I would never have done that to you. Friends are supposed to be there for each other, regardless of what is happening in each other's lives. But you aren't a real friend, are you, Abraham? You are one of those fair weather variety, only around when the going is good."

"How can you say that?" His voice was raised. "I have always been there for you, looking out for you when we were at school! I have been a better friend to you than most. The only time I have turned away from you was when I thought you were leaving me!"

He was panting. Rachel felt tears welling, again. What was the point of this? They couldn't communicate, anymore. They had grown so far away from each other. It was sad, but it couldn't be mended, obviously.

"The blizzard has cleared," she said. "I think you need to leave, Abraham."

She walked past him, refusing to look at him.

No, she had no idea of anything, anymore. She had lost two people who she had thought were friends. One of them she had been losing for a while, anyway; it had been a band aid she had been frightened to rip off, for fear of the pain. But in the end, she got the pain anyway. The other was a quick pain that would keep hurting, for a while at least.

There was no avoiding pain, that was obvious. You might try to dodge it, walk around it, or ignore it, but it would follow you, whether you liked it or not.

She prayed silently as she walked. She had been full of confusion about her life, and what she would do. At least now, one path was gone. She would not be keen to experience the English world, again. She was out of her depth, and besides, the incident with David had made her realise how dear her world was to her. She didn't want to lose it; not now, not ever.

She would talk to her father. She had made her decision; she wanted to be baptized into the faith.

She thought of Abraham. No, he hadn't followed her. She knew he wouldn't. He had made his choice, a long time ago. And she didn't want to be friends with someone, anyway, who couldn't accept her for herself. The good sides of her, as well as the bad.

It was all for the best.

***

Rachel sat beside her best friend Lovina. It felt good to re-connect with her. She hadn't seen her in a long time, since she had been busy with David.

The two girls were inside, next to the blazing fire. The roads had finally opened, and Christmas had come and gone. Lovina had called around to Rachel's house to deliver her Christmas present.

Rachel's eyes shone when she ripped open the small present. In her lap was a handmade crocheted rug. Rachel threw her arms around her friend.

"Thank you," she whispered, tears in her eyes. She hadn't lost all her friends.

"You're welcome," Lovina said, smiling. She had already opened Rachel's present to her, a knitted scarf. It was wound around her neck.

"You can take it off, you know," Rachel said, gesturing to the scarf. "It must be hot wearing it inside!"

The two girls laughed. Then Lovina looked at her friend. She could tell something was bothering her.

"How is David?" she asked, gently. It was as she thought. At the mere mention of the name, Rachel bristled and blushed.

"What happened, Rachel?" Lovina took her friend's hand.

"Oh," Rachel tried to smile. "We had an argument. He thought something that wasn't true about me, and didn't believe me when I told him he was wrong. It doesn't matter."

"I thought that might be the case," said Lovina, looking at her friend tenderly. "Dear Rachel, you are so shy and unsure around men. Sometimes, they misunderstand things. Especially in the English world, or so I have been told." She paused, looking at Rachel. "Have you made a decision? Do you want to stay in the faith?"

"I do," answered Rachel. It felt like a weight was lifted off her shoulders, just saying the words. She felt lighter, somehow.

Yes, the incident with David had been the catalyst, but it was more than that. God had shown her all that she stood to lose if she embraced the English world. As far as Rachel was concerned, the price was far too high to pay.

"I am so happy," said Lovina. She clutched Rachel's hands, tears in her eyes. "I don't know what I would have done without you. And I know that I am not the only one who feels that way, Rachel."

"What do you mean?"

"I am talking about Abraham." Lovina looked at her friend, gauging her reaction. "He has been so troubled, watching your forays into the English world."

Rachel scoffed. "I think you are mistaken, Lovina. Abraham doesn't care for me, any longer. He made that very clear after the blizzard. He was never a real friend."

"Rachel, how can you be so dense?" Lovina looked at her friend, her eyes widening. "It's because he is a real friend that he was so concerned! But there is more to it than that. I think he has stronger feelings for you, Rachel."

"What?" Rachel looked at her friend as if she had just started talking in another language. She shook her head, vigorously. "No, you are mistaken. If he felt that way about me, why wouldn't he have told me? And why would he just cut me off?"

"Because he was hurt, Rachel," Lovina replied. "He thought you were rejecting our faith and him, in the process. It was too much for him; he felt like he had to turn away completely." Lovina glanced sideways at Rachel. "That's what I believe, anyway."

"No, you are wrong," said Rachel, frowning.

She stood up. "I might just get a glass of water," she said. She walked to the kitchen, thinking deeply.

Lovina's words were swimming around in her brain. They made no sense to her. It was as if her world had tilted sideways. Could it be true?

And how did she feel, if it was? Abraham had been a constant in her life, as stable as the sun and the moon in the sky to her. She had assumed that he would be there, forever. It had hurt her immeasurably when he had withdrawn from her. As if the sun had dimmed, and the moon had stopped shedding its luminescence.

As if her world had stopped.

***

At least her parents were happy. That was something.

Rachel had told them her decision to join the faith, and they had been overjoyed.

"We were so worried about you," said her mother. "We thought there was a strong chance that you would join the English world." She had clasped her daughter's hands, her eyes full of tears.

Her father had nodded, pleased. "I always knew you would make the right decision," he said. "Rachel, the world is full of wonders. But your place is here, with us. I am glad that God has shown you the right path."

She was feeling a bit better about the incident with David. She accepted it for what it was, and that she had misjudged him. She had been swept away by the world he offered, for a little while. It was as simple as that.

Now that she had made her decision, everything was clear. Except, maybe, what had happened with Abraham.

She realised that she loved him. She always had. But he had turned away from her, so there was no hope for them, now. If only she had realised sooner. Maybe they might have had a chance.

Rachel walked to the end of their property, thinking deeply. She was happy that she was going to be baptised, but she was also sad. Sad for a lost love, that had never developed.

She heard a noise behind her, and turned around. The snow was still deep; although the sky was clear, she hadn't expected anyone else to be out here.

A dark figure loomed before her. She had to blink twice, thinking that she had conjured him from her imagination.

For in front of her was Abraham.

Yes, it was really him.

"Rachel." He walked toward her, not smiling. "Your mother told me you were out here, taking a walk." He paused, struggling for words. "I need to talk to you. I feel that you have misunderstood me, and I can't stop thinking about it."

She looked at him, snowflakes brushing his dark winter overcoat and black hat. Her heart swelled. If she could stand here, like this, forever, just looking at him, she would be happy.

"Abraham." She stared into his eyes. Was it possible? Were Lovina's words true?

Abraham sighed, deeply. "Will you walk with me?"

"Of course," she said.

They turned and started walking, together. She glanced at him sideways, trying to judge his mood. But he was still silent, gathering his thoughts.

Eventually, he stopped and turned.

"I know it is useless," he blurted. "But it doesn't matter to me, anymore. I have tried for so long to stop feeling this way. I know that you don't feel the same way. But I can't deny it. I have to at least tell you."

Rachel's heart stopped, just for a moment. Her breath caught on the cold wind.

"Rachel, I love you," he said, his eyes pleading. "I have loved you forever, and I will never stop loving you. I haven't told you, because I saw that you weren't ready. You needed to go off and explore the world. I was trying to give you space, to find yourself."

"Oh, Abraham," she gasped. "I had no idea. I was so hurt when you refused to be my friend, any longer. I just couldn't understand."

"It hurt me too much," he whispered, "to see you. Knowing that I loved you. And then when you started seeing David, I thought that was it. There was no chance at all." He paused, taking a deep breath. "I wanted to respect your decision. Even though I knew that he didn't deserve you."

Rachel's eyes filled with tears. "Abraham," she whispered back. "I was confused. I wasn't sure where I belonged. But I have made up my mind, now. My place is here, in our community."

He smiled, for the first time that day. It was beautiful to her. "I am so glad," he said.

"And my place is with you," she continued, facing him. "I am sorry it has taken me so long to realise it. I love you, too, Abraham. I always have, and I always will."

His smile spread wider across his face. His eyes glimmered with tears. "It is more than I hoped for. I can't tell you how many times I have dreamed of this moment." He paused. "Rachel, will you be my wife?"

The tears that had been threatening spilled over. "Oh Abraham, nothing in this world would make me happier," she breathed.

Her heart was overflowing.

It had taken her a while, to get here. To find her place in her community, and realise her love. But it had been worth it, the journey. She wouldn't take back a moment of it; not the soul searching, or the confusion. She wouldn't even take back what had happened with David.

Because it had all led her here, to this moment. As God had planned, all along.

THE END